Frontier Justice

When a man is drawn by love, crushed by death, and driven by revenge, he can't wait for justice on the 1840 frontier. It is left for him to deliver it with a Colt Dragoon.

James Oliver Virmala

Edition 2

Cover Photo By James Oliver Virmala

ISBN: 978-0-9972536-5-8

DEDICATION

This book is dedicated to our military men and women. They spend long periods of time away from their loved ones separated from the touch, taste, and smell of those left behind while depending on their spouses to be both mother and father in their children's lives.

CONTENTS

BOOKS BY THE AUTHOR

Oli's Gold Book One
Search For Oli's Gold Book Two
Return To Oli's Gold Book Three
To Be A Mountain Man
Trouble On The Kansas Plains
Frontier Justice
Return Of The Mountain Man
The Tall Man
The Prospector
The Green Valley
Twilight Of The Mountain Man
The Mother Lode
Quest Of The Mountain Man
Journey's End
Rufus Pike
Rufus And The Pup
The Winding Trail Home
Rufus The Lost Years
The Kankakee Kid
Bogus Island
Tyler Tomas The Brothers' War
War of 1812 The Choice

CHAPTER ONE

The midday sun blazed down on the sweat-stained man as he led the lame horse along Little Bear Creek. It was a warm summer day in 1849. Several miles back, the man's buckskin had begun to favor the front left leg. A quick inspection had revealed a loose shoe. To prevent further damage, Bart Nevell chose to lead the horse the rest of the way to Fort Graham.

He was a tall man with broad shoulders. He wore a faded, gray wool shirt and army trousers tucked into his well-worn boots. A knife handle protruded from the right boot top. There was a Hawken .53 caliber rifle with a single trigger and 33-inch barrel in the saddle scabbard. He carried a .44 caliber Colt Dragoon revolver in an open holster on his right side.

Adjusting his flat-brimmed hat, he squinted at the small cabin visible downriver. The rocky terrain around him was covered with mesquite, cat claw and red cedar. Groves of live oak with their spreading branches offered shade for the weary traveler. The weathered log building was surrounded by massive oaks.

Leading the tired buckskin to a spring next to the cabin, he wrapped the reins around a large fallen branch. The grateful horse dipped its nose into the pool of water and drank deeply. Stepping back, Bart stretched his weary back and looked around for any sign of activity near the building. The spring flowed across the front of the structure, past a split pole corral and eventually meandered down to Little Bear Creek.

Taking his canteen from the saddle, the tall man poured out the tepid water and dipped it into the fresh water of the spring. Taking a satisfying drink from the canteen, he then filled it to the top. Hanging the canteen back onto the saddle, he returned to the spring and rinsed his dirt-streaked face and red-rimmed eyes.

Reaching into his saddle bag, Bart retrieved a piece of elk jerky and some hard bread. He thought briefly about making a small fire for coffee, but decided against it and filled his cup with cool water instead. Sitting on the thick, broken branch, he began to chew his midday meal and sip water.

Smiling, he looked at the horse now grazing on grass alongside the spring. "Enjoy your meal, Buck. We got another couple hours walk before we get you to a blacksmith." Other than a twitch of its ears, the animal made little response to the man's voice.

Grunting, Bart stood up and stuck the last piece of bread into his mouth. Drinking the remaining water to soften the bread, he chewed slowly as he walked toward the cabin. The horse had been ridden steadily since leaving Kansas. It also carried supplies from the pack horse, which had been stolen by Indians.

Out of habit, he stopped short of the dwelling

and studied the area. There were tracks that were several days old in front of the cabin. Four or five horses had been tied to the makeshift rail for several hours. Empty rye bottles littered the ground. A gust of wind carried the scent of rotting meat. He snorted to try and get the smell out of his nose.

Muttering, "The drunks must've butchered a deer or beef," he pulled the sagging door open.

The loud buzz of flies met him along with the sickening smell of two rotting corpses lying in the middle of the floor. The dead men wore army uniforms. Their heads and shoulders were badly torn up by what appeared to be shotgun blasts.

Bart stepped back quickly, shocked by what he had found. Sucking deeply of air outside the cabin, he stepped back in, holding his breath as he looked around. Stepping back out, he leaned against the peeling logs, thinking about what he had found. He was no stranger to the savagery that one could find on the frontier.

For years he had worked as a scout for the army, seeing unthinkable acts done by men on all sides. He had scouted for wagon trains, hunted buffalo, tracked men, and killed his share while doing so. There had been a woman he had met in Texas some years ago whom he had promised to come back to. The promise had been an idle one. Drinking had always been Bart's weakness. The woman had nursed him back to health after a two-week drunk. He had been beaten by a group of men who had gotten tired of his rowdy behavior in their Texas saloon.

Earlier this past summer he had let a friend down, almost causing the man's death. He vowed then to stop drinking and go back to find the woman in

Texas. He had come into some money and planned to purchase a small ranch and start a family.

Bart realized that he could not leave the two bodies of the soldiers unburied. A shovel hung on the shack wall. Taking it down, he walked back to the buckskin and moved it to fresh grass. Removing the bit, he staked it out with a picket rope. "It looks like we'll be spending the night here, Buck."

Hefting the shovel, he walked behind the cabin and struggled to dig two graves in the rocky soil. Finishing the digging, his shirt damp with sweat, Bart then wrapped the bodies in the rodent-chewed blankets from a bunk and lowered them into the holes. Filling them with dirt and stacking rocks over the graves, he then stepped back and removed his hat. With head bowed, he did his best to say the right words over the men. He thought of his old friend, Oli. He seemed to have a knack for knowing what to say.

He had found little in the men's pockets. A leather money belt lay next to the bodies with a letter addressed to one of them. Any money it may have held was gone. If the soldiers had carried weapons, they had been taken along with their horses.

It was late afternoon by the time the men were buried. Years of scouting and tracking men were ingrained in Bart and he took time to make a thorough search of the area for any clues as to who may have been at the cabin. Leading his horse back to the stream, he set up camp. He would get an early start for the fort in the morning. If he left now, it would be after dark before he arrived.

CHAPTER TWO

Bart kept supper simple. He fried his remaining bacon over a small fire. He roasted and crushed the last of his coffee beans and split the results so there would be enough left for the morning. Looking at his horse he said, "Good thing we are getting to the fort tomorrow. I would get mighty hungry on what we have left."

The horse ignored him and kept cropping grass. "Damn poor company you are, Buck."

With the meal complete, he checked the buckskin's leg. A small stone had jammed under the shoe. Using his knife, he pried it loose. He hoped the stone had not caused any bruising to the hoof. He then rubbed the horse down with dried grass. Watering it once more, he picketed it close to his camp and the spring.

Bart laughed as he watched the horse roll. "See if I comb your hide again if you're just going to mess it up."

By dark he had the fire banked and his bed roll

spread out. The sky was clear, indicating a cool night, but no rain. It was mid-July. The fort he was heading for had just been established. Word from contacts at Fort Leavenworth was that Fort Graham was to be an observation post to keep an eye on the many tribes west and north of it.

After Bart watched the stars crawl across the sky for an hour, the moon rose, masking their brightness. The night sky had always been interesting to Bart. How far up the stars were and what caused some to fall were always mysteries. With heavy eyelids, he settled into his blankets.

The sound of the buckskin snorting brought him wide awake. Lying still, he listened to the night sounds. The position of the stars told him it was well after midnight. The area was bathed in moonlight. Bart didn't know what had startled the horse. The animal was staring toward the cabin, ears pricked forward.

There was the creak of a saddle. Someone had swung down from a horse. He heard the sound of metal against metal. He was now sure that the noise was coming from the far side of the building. Bart knew that sound would carry in the still coolness of the night. With care, he rose from his blankets and pulled his revolver from under his saddle. The heaviness of the Colt Dragoon in his hand was comforting.

Someone was near the cabin, and by what he was hearing probably up to no good. In his long underwear and stocking feet, he calmed his horse. Bart moved silently to the back of the cabin. The smell of lamp oil was strong. A can clunked on the ground. There was the strike of flint on steel. The unknown man was lighting a fire to burn the cabin!

Running around the side of the cabin with his Dragoon raised, Bart shouted, "What the hell are you doing?"

The man leaped back as though shot. Howling in fear, the man ran and grabbed for his horse. It sidestepped and he fell headlong onto the ground. Still crying like the devil was after him, he rolled over and drew his revolver, firing wildly into the night.

One of the bullets chipped wood from a post near Bart, sending stinging splinters into his cheek. Lining up the .44 caliber on the man, he squeezed off a shot. The thunder of the shot and the terrified screams of the man ceased, except for fading echoes from the hills. The man's horse stomped nervously, pulling at the tied reins.

The shot from the Colt Dragoon went true through the man's heart. He lay with his arms spread wide, eyes staring sightlessly into the night. Bart had been lucky. The man had just lit the cabin and the blaze had left him with night blindness. When Bart's large, light-colored figure had appeared around the side of the cabin, the dead man probably thought he was seeing one of the soldiers' ghosts.

"You poor bastard," he said to the man. "You were trying to destroy the evidence of the killings and ended up shot yourself."

Walking past him, he kicked the man's boot with his stocking foot to make sure there was no life left in him. Speaking softly, he quieted the horse. Fortunately, the reins were tied in a tight knot, preventing the lunging animal from pulling free.

"You're a good-looking mustang." The horse reached its head out, seeking comfort from Bart.

Leading the horse back to the spring, he tied it

to the fallen branch. As he turned away, the horse nuzzled him as though to say thank you. Bart looked at his buckskin, which was ignoring them while grazing.

"You, Buck, could take some lessons from this animal."

It was still several hours before daylight. The flames were quickly devouring the weathered structure. He doubted sleep would come again. Plucking the burrs from his socks, he wondered about the man he had just shot. Dressing quickly, he scooped some embers from the burning cabin and added them to his small fire. He then put water on for coffee.

Daylight found him sitting against the live oak, drinking the last of the brew and watching the smoldering remains of the building. The dead fire starter lay where Bart had left him. Getting up stiffly, Bart moved just beyond the oak and relieved himself of some of the coffee. It was time to get started for the fort. Bart tied the body across the rump of the horse and then settled into the saddle in front of it.

The mustang moved eagerly along the trail despite the weight of two men on its back. The buckskin followed, walking gingerly on the bad shoe. A search of the man's pockets had revealed a marked deck of cards, a few personal items, some tobacco, and nearly $50 on the man. His clothing was typical range wear. He had not intended spending the night and carried nothing to camp with.

Whether the man had killed the soldiers, or had been sent by someone else to fire the cabin was unknown. Bart had decided to bring the body to the fort and make them aware of what he found, leaving it for them to figure out. After a quick stop at Fort

Graham for supplies, he would be heading down the Brazos River, an hour's ride, to a newly established place called Waco Village.

It was named after the Waco tribe that had once inhabited the area. Situated on the west bank of the Brazos, it boasted a cold, clear spring that could satisfy the thirstiest resident or traveler. The lady of his quest worked at a saloon and trading post named Wolfgang's, less than a mile from the spring. Its owner had chosen the location because it offered the best river crossing.

Fort Graham came into view at mid-morning. The fort consisted of log and clapboard buildings. Bart had expected it to be larger. It did offer a commissary, livery, blacksmith shop, and a hospital. He passed the blacksmith shop first. Throwing his leg over the mustang's head, he slid to the ground. The smithy stopped in mid-swing at the shoe he was working on when he saw the big man with a body draped across the back of the saddle.

"I got me a lame horse here. I think it's only a loose shoe," he explained to the smithy.

"Is that a dead man you got there?" the surprised smithy asked.

"Yep. Don't worry, he is not going anywhere. I figured the buckskin needed tending to first."

Wiping his massive hands on his leather apron, he walked up and took the reins of the horse. Pointing to the body, "You best take 'im over to Major Arnold's office," the smithy advised. "Killed by Indians?" he asked.

"Nope, by me," Bart said, and then headed for the headquarters leading the mustang and its owner.

The smell of freshly hewed logs was strong in

the major's headquarters. The sound of axes, saws, and hammers were a constant din. Construction of the fort had been going at a fast pace since spring. The parade ground was clean and neat, which would be expected, while the road to and from the fort was rutted and wet in the swampy areas and bumpy and dust-covered elsewhere.

Furnishings in the front office were sparse. A private in an ill-fitting uniform sat at the desk. His youthfulness surprised Bart. Maybe seeing the lad made him feel even older than he'd like to admit.

The private looked up and smiled. "Can I help you, mister?"

"Got the body of a fellow I had to shoot outside."

The smile faded from the young man's face and his eyes widened. "A body . . . ah, you'd better show it to me."

He followed Bart out the door and looked at the dead man draped over the horse. "Shit whiskers, I think I know the man."

"You do?" Bart asked.

"Well, not by name, but he come into town with the boys from the Bar G ranch. That's old man Gerber's place."

"Axel Gerber?" Bart's brow rose at hearing the name. "He and his son, a boy about your age, had one of the biggest spreads around."

"One and the same," the private confirmed. "He won't like having his men shot."

"Well, the horse and the body must be Gerber's. If you don't mind, I will leave them with you."

"What the hell is going on there?" The inquiry

came from the street. A stocky lieutenant with a bushy moustache stood staring at the body.

The young private snapped to attention. "Sir, this man brought in a man he killed."

Shaking his head, the lieutenant snapped, "Private, get him the hell off the street and have someone put up the horse." Pointing at Bart, he continued. "You, come in my office."

Bart followed the man back into the headquarters. He headed for one of the offices on the left. The lieutenant muttered as he walked. "Damn recruits don't know enough to get out of the sun. He'd have let the damn body rot before he moved it."

Walking into his office, the lieutenant tossed his hat onto a hook and sat heavily in a sturdy chair behind his desk.

Motioning to a chair in front of the desk, he said, "I'm Lieutenant Riddle. Have a seat, Nevell."

The big man was shocked to hear his name spoken. "You . . . you know me?"

"Hell, I've been around this man's army longer than I care to think about."

Suddenly sneezing, the lieutenant pulled a soiled handkerchief from his pocket and gave his nose a good blow. Mopping back his now slightly wet moustache, he looked up at Bart.

"It was about 10 years ago at Fort Gibson. I was still green to the west and you were already scouting for the army. I don't expect you to remember me, but you sure as hell impressed me."

Embarrassed at the compliment, Bart brought up the bodies in the cabin to change the subject. "You might be missing a couple of your troops. I found two shot in a cabin a few hours' ride up Bear Creek."

He reached inside his shirt and brought out the wallet and letter. "Found these in the room. If they had any weapons, they were gone. Looked like someone used a shotgun, tore them up something awful. I buried the men. That night, the fellow I brought in burnt the cabin. When I challenged him, he started shooting and I shot back. I think he thought I was a ghost of one of the dead soldiers."

The lieutenant stared at the letter while Bart spoke. Throwing it back onto his desk, he snorted. "Damn. Damn this to hell. We were missing two men." He picked the letter back up and shook it. "This here was Wells' and the other would have been Keller. They have been missing for four days."

Lieutenant Riddle stood up and walked over to the window and looked up the street. "We are short-handed enough as it is. We cannot afford to lose men with experience like Wells and Keller."

Bart sat uncomfortably and wanted to get on his way. "May have been a card game gone bad. Course, it would be a long way to ride for cards when they could play around here."

"The men couldn't play around here. The major was having too much trouble with low lives taking the soldiers' money in crooked games and made card playing off-limits," the lieutenant said.

Bart felt impatient to head downriver. Standing, he said, "Well, I got to go pick up my horse and a few supplies and be on my way."

"You know, Nevell, we sure could use you around here. We need a good scout," Lieutenant Riddle said.

"Had my belly full of army life. I got me a little bit of money and want to put down some roots."

Disappointment was obvious on the lieutenant's face. "If you change your mind, the offer stands. I do need you to set with the private out there and give him a brief account of what happened."

It was mid-afternoon before he made it back to the blacksmith shop. His stomach burned with hunger and he was feeling aggravated at the delay caused by doing the proper thing. The young private's eyes glowed with excitement as he took down the information. One would think he was writing for one of the eastern newspapers, based on the number of questions he asked.

The smithy was sitting on a block of wood in front of his shop when Bart walked up. "Just finished shoeing your horse and am taking a water break."

The big man was surprised at the amount of time it took. "Was the lame hoof in that bad shape?"

"Naw," the sweaty and soot-covered man said. "Had a few things to finish for Alex's boy. He gets a might testy if his work isn't done first thing. Your horse is as good as new."

Settling with the blacksmith for shoeing the buckskin, Bart swung into the saddle. "Where can I get a meal around here?"

"Not much in the fort at this time of day. About 20 minutes downriver is a cantina run by a fellow whose wife makes decent grub." With business concluded, the smithy turned and headed back into his shop.

Bart decided to put off getting more supplies at the fort and start downriver. He hoped to be sitting with a large plate with frijoles refritos in front of him shortly. The cantina was a low, gleaming, white building with adobe walls and a clay tiled roof, undoubtedly built when Mexico claimed the area. An arching doorway led into a shaded, cool, inviting room. The sound of laughter was heard inside as he swung down from Buck.

"Take care of your horse, señor?" a slight, young Mexican boy said as he hurried from around the cantina.

The hot afternoon sun burned down and getting the horse into the shade was a good idea. "If you water him and get him some grain."

"Si, señor, I will even brush him if the price is right." The beaming boy's teeth were white against his dark skin.

Tossing a coin to the young man, he walked into the cantina. The smell of tequila, chili peppers, and sweat lingered in the room. Four cowboys sat playing cards on a hand-made plank table to one side near an open window.

A stocky Mexican with a thin, carefully trimmed moustache leaned against a badly scarred bar that had seen better days.

"Can I get something to eat?" Bart inquired.

"I'll have Benita get you something. You want some tequila to wash the dust down?"

"Got any coffee or tea?" Bart asked.

Looking at the big man, he said, sarcastically, "Benita will heat water for your tea."

Disappearing for a moment behind a beaded curtain, he returned and moved down the bar after glancing at the big man.

Bart chose a table near the door. The smell and sense of the place felt too good. His throat ached for the familiar burn of the alcohol. The air from outside was necessary to save him from having that first drink.

He watched with envy as the man behind the bar brought a fresh bottle of tequila to the cowboys' table. The bartender said something to the group, which caused a chorus of laughter as they glanced his way.

Being the brunt of a joke was not something Bart took well. He felt a smoldering anger begin to build inside. He was about to get up and confront the four when a short, heavyset woman pushed through the beaded curtain carrying a platter of tortillas filled with thick frijoles, a pitcher, and a cup.

Setting them heavily in front of him, she said, "Ignore them, señor. They are drunk. I have made you a fine meal and a pitcher of something better than hot tea."

The smell of the food and his empty stomach made him quickly forget the cowboys. He wolfed down one of the tortillas before filling his cup with the pitcher. The drink was cool and sweet and tasted of lemon or orange.

In short order, he had the platter of food eaten and was leaning his stool back against the wall while he sipped the last of the drink. He had all but forgotten about the four men and was ready to go find his horse.

He suddenly became aware of someone standing over him. He looked up into the sneering face of one of the cowboys.

"My name's Dieter Gerber, tea drinker."

"You growed up, boy. You best step back or you won't get any older," Bart warned.

Confused by the response, Gerber stood stupidly for a moment.

"You heard me boy, step back." In a fluid motion, the big man stood and shoved the young cowboy back. The boy tripped over his own feet and fell heavily onto the dirt floor.

The other three men stood, knocking their stools over. As they turned, they froze, staring into the deadly barrel of the Colt Dragoon.

"Don't do something stupid. I already had to kill one of your friends and won't hesitate to shoot one or all of you." The cold, deadly stare from Bart convinced them to abandon any ideas that they might have had.

Lying on the floor, Dieter shouted at them, "Get him, you damn cowards! He killed Len."

Bart reached down and grabbed the fallen cowboy by the shirt and lifted him with one hand, his boots barely touching the floor. After slamming him against the wall, he then shoved him in the direction of his friends. Once again, he tripped and fell headlong across the table, spreading the cards and money on the floor.

The others stood focused on the gun and had little desire to move to the aid of Dieter. Dropping a coin onto the table to pay for his meal, he glanced at the bartender, who was leaning as if uninterested against the bar. Bart noticed that one arm was out of sight, probably holding a club or other weapon.

"I had no intention of causing you any trouble. Tell the lady that the meal and drink was most satisfying." Then, to the cowboys he said, "I am leaving now. If you follow me out the door I will take it as a challenge and shoot."

He found the young Mexican boy around back of the cantina. He was just finishing putting the saddle back onto the buckskin after currying the animal. The horse was still licking at the wooden bucket the grain was in.

Turning quickly and giving Bart a broad smile, he patted the shoulder of the buckskin. "It is a very good horse, señor. He listens well and must be a good companion on the trail."

Thanking the young man and checking the cinch strap before mounting, he turned Buck down the trail. "You sure got the young fellow buffaloed, don't you, horse?"

The buckskin walked on, ignoring his master's words.

CHAPTER THREE

Bart was bigger than most men, with broad, well-muscled shoulders and arms. His rugged face had a natural scowl, which gave people the impression that he was angry. The occasional traveler he passed while riding down the winding trail along the Brazos River would be left with that impression, but inside Bart's emotions were far different.

He could feel the rising excitement of returning to the only place he thought of as home. Landmarks in the area were familiar. The alder brush and black oak trees lined the trail. The smell and feel of the area brought back a flood of memories, some bad, but others very good.

One of the best was the soft, healing hands of a blond saloon gal named Millie. For two weeks, she had nursed his bruised and battered body back to health. They had continued to see each other until he'd headed west to look for work scouting. He had left her with a promise to come back when he had a stake and marry her.

The dusty streets of Waco had been the bed of the drunken Bart many nights in the past when he had been unable to stagger to the livery. He stopped at the cold spring and took a long, refreshing drink. Wiping his mouth with the back of his hand, he looked down the slope toward his destination.

Swinging back onto the buckskin, he rode away from the spring and glanced up at the large log cabin situated on the bluff above the spring. It was said that the first white child in this area had been born there.

Bart urged the horse on, knowing that within the hour he would be seeing Millie again. He wished that he had taken time to bathe and shave. The delay at the fort had forced him to change his plans. He was sure that Millie would look past his four-day beard and dusty appearance.

He had Buck at a trot as he approached Wolfgang's. The condition of the two-section building was worse than he remembered. Swinging down from the buckskin, he tied it to the broken hitching post. Quickly, he strode across the plank walk and into the open door of the saloon.

It was late afternoon and he had expected to find it busy with men having a drink before heading home. The dim and dusty front room had a plank bar against the right wall. Tables with stools or chairs were on the left side. Various goods were piled on the shelves and tables in the back room. The saloon floor was worn planks covered with clumps of clay from boots and sawdust. Heavy cobwebs of wolf spiders stretched across the hand-hewed ceiling beams.

The sound of Bart's boots on the floor boards brought the owner from the back room. "Welcome to Wolfgang's," he bellowed.

The voice echoed in the empty room. Bart walked up to the bar and placed both hands on the edge of the planks. "I'm here to see Millie."

The man, wearing a dirty white shirt and sagging woolen britches, cocked his head and looked at Bart. "She ain't here no more. Hey, ain't you Bart Nevell?"

"Yep, I am back and looking for Millie."

Looking at the big man, the owner shook his head. "She's gone with the rest of my customers. They've all gone up to Waco. The river boats can't pull in here cause it's too shallow. They pull in at the landing in Waco. A couple of new saloons opened up there and took all my business. I get a little trade with the Mexicans and Indians."

He turned to grab a bottle of rye off the back bar. "I got rye, or rye to drink." All he heard in reply were the heavy footsteps of Bart heading for the buckskin.

Swinging into the saddle, he turned the horse back towards Waco. "Another damn waste of time," he muttered.

He saw several horses tied up in front of the Mustang Saloon as he arrived back in Waco. The sound of laughter and a piano greeted him on the street. Finding room on the hitching rail, he swung down from the buckskin and loosened the cinch.

Slapping the horse on the rump, he said, "I won't be too long, Buck. Wish me luck."

Hopping up on the board walk in front of the saloon, he pushed open the batwing doors and stepped into the cool, dim room. He closed his eyes briefly and took in the scent of the whisky, beer, perfume, and sweat.

His first impulse was to step up to the bar and order a stiff shot, but he fought the urge and moved to the center of the room. The bar was lined with cowboys and shop keepers. Three tables had men playing poker.

It took a moment for Bart to locate Millie. His spirits rose and fell as quickly. Millie was down at the end of the bar, sharing a drink with Dieter Gerber. He had his arm around her waist, pulling her toward him.

Bart felt the heat of anger rise as he watched her laugh and make a feeble attempt to push him away. Fighting down the notion of going over and interrupting the little party, he moved over to a table and sat facing the street.

He knew that she was only doing her job, something he had seen many times before. He also realized that part of her job and income was to persuade a tipsy cowboy to join her in one of the back rooms. Somehow these memories of Millie had been lost during his long absence.

His dark mood was broken by dainty footsteps and the smell of sweet perfume. "Can I get you something, cowboy?"

Turning quickly, he looked into the dark eyes of a plump, brown-haired young woman. "I'll have a beer," he replied, obvious disappointment on his face.

"Buy me a drink? I've been looking for a strong man like you."

He felt her hand on his shoulder. Pressing a coin into her hand, he replied, "Just a beer, you keep the rest for yourself."

Bart wasn't accustomed to throwing money at dance hall girls, but he knew that she would continue to work him until she got something.

The young woman returned with his beer and started to sit. "If you don't mind, I want to be alone." Pretending to be offended, she moved away from his table and toward the bar to find an easier customer.

The beer was warm and unsatisfying. Bart knew better than to switch to rye. One drink was never enough. He sipped the yeasty brew and stared at the door, trying his best to shut out the sounds of merriment behind him.

The steps of several men came up behind him. He turned his head away as they passed. He feared that Millie might be leaving with them. Glancing back at the men, he recognized the swaggering step of Dieter leading some of his sidekicks. Quick steps followed them, stopping short of the door.

"Come back later boys, I'll be here," Millie called to the departing men. Turning back to find a new opportunity, her eyes fell on the big man.

For a second, there was no recognition. Then her eyes opened wide and she shrieked, "Bart!" With emotions gone wild, she ran and jumped into his lap, throwing her arms around him, hugging him tightly.

"You said you would come back. I didn't believe it, but here you are."

A man of little emotion other than anger, Bart held her awkwardly as she snuggled in his lap. "Millie, I told you I would come back."

Sitting back and holding him at arm's length, she squealed, "This calls for a drink."

As she tried to stand up, he pulled her back down. "I got me a beer, Millie. I best stick with that."

Confused, she looked at him. "You ain't sick are you, Bart?" she asked.

"Drinking may be the only sickness I got. I

come back for you," he replied.

She pushed herself away and sat on the chair opposite him. "I ain't available, Bart. You don't want someone like me. At least not like you're saying."

Lost for a way to explain how he felt, he leaned over the table and struggled for the right words. "I know how you have made a living. You know how I have lived, often cleaning stables to earn enough for a bottle. Being thrown out of places into the street, and being too drunk to crawl out of the horseshit I was laying in."

"Don't talk about yourself like that," she scolded.

"Nothing I'm saying is untrue. It took letting down a good friend and almost getting him killed that opened my eyes. I finally got a little money ahead. I want to buy some land and a few cows or horses and make a life for you and me."

He looked into her tear-filled eyes. Uttering, "No," she stood up and walked to the piano, pretending to listen.

Bart, unsure what more he could say, sat wondering what her final answer would be. He looked over, knowing he should follow her. He was about to stand up when she walked quickly to the bar and started talking to one of the businessmen.

He stared at the half-finished beer. Flexing and un-flexing his fists, he felt helpless. He did not want to believe her walking away was the end. The sound of her laughter made his muscles jump.

Sweeping the beer off the table with the back of his hand, it crashed to the floor. Bart stood up, knocking the table over. He wanted to hurt someone. In the worst way he wanted to inflict pain on another to ease his own.

The men at the bar near him moved back, away from the raging hulk of a man. Millie moved behind the man she was talking to. Fear showed in her eyes. Seeing that shook Bart.

Stumbling blindly out into the sunlight, he missed the end of the walk and fell against the hitching rail. The buckskin snorted and pulled back. Steadying himself against the rail, he stood with his legs shaking. He never remembered feeling so weak.

Tightening the cinch, he climbed into the saddle. Turning the horse, he rode back towards Wolfgang's. He knew that he should forget everything that had just happened and move on, but he wasn't ready to give up just yet.

As the big man rode south, his broad shoulders slumping, he missed seeing Millie watch him go, tears streaming down her face.

CHAPTER FOUR

Wolfgang was walking out of the trading post door with an axe in his hand as Bart rode up. He looked up and in his booming voice, asked, "You back for that drink?"

During the slow ride from Waco, Bart had regained some of his composure. His head was still spinning from the meeting. A plan of going forward had not developed. "Much as I'd like a drink, I got some thinking to do. I could use a room and a meal."

"Let me finish splitting some wood and I'll cook something up. Got a loft in the back you can use. Four bits will get you the bed and chow."

"Bart dismounted and walked up, taking the axe from Wolfgang. "Let me split the wood. I need to work off some anger."

Taking the axe, Bart laid into the wood, taking huge aggressive swings, sending chips flying. It felt good to sweat. Soon, several days' firewood laid cut. The owner emerged from a side door and beamed when he saw the pile.

"Next time you need to work off some anger, just stop by."

Bart stripped the gear from the buckskin. Placing it on the porch in front of the saloon, he led the horse around the back of the building where Wolfgang had a lean-to. He forked some hay in for the buckskin and gave it a quick rubdown.

He then went back into the building, where he found the owner cooking beef steaks in a large black frying pan. A pot of yesterday's beans was warming on the back of the stove.

"Bring your gear into the loft. Supper is about ready."

The loft had a low ceiling and Bart had to duck the rafters as he moved around. The cot had a hay tick mattress supported by leather strapping. His feet would hang over the end of the short bed.

Climbing down the ladder from the loft, he joined Wolfgang at a large wooden table in the saloon. The steaks took some chewing, but were tasty. The beans had some kind of pepper that left his mouth burning.

Bart drank coffee while Wolfgang tossed down shots of tequila. "You ain't no fun being sober," the owner said.

"You must have liked to fix your furniture. I sure remember busting lots of it up," Bart laughed.

"Ya, that you did. But you sure brought the cowboys in. They all wanted a piece of you. Having you drunk was good for business."

Leaning back in his chair, Bart looked at Wolfgang over the brim of his mug. "You know of any places for sale? Not too big, maybe 500 to a 1,000 acres."

"What you want to grow, corn or beans?" the owner asked.

"Either cows or horses are my plans."

"Well, heard that old man Dabney died and his son is trying to turn the farm into quick cash. He may even have a couple head on the property."

Bart remembered the Dabney spread from the past. He had fair grazing and water on the property. He had ridden across it while hunting once. He had met Charles Dabney working his cattle. As he recalled, the man had been a proper Englishman.

"I never knew he had a son," Bart said.

"Not here he didn't. The boy grew up in Boston with his mother. Old man Dabney left them behind. She refused to move west. Believe he sent her money regular like any good Englishman would do."

Having shared this knowledge with Bart, Wolfgang began cleaning up the supper dishes. Pouring another cup of coffee, the big man let him do it. He figured that at a dollar a day, he shouldn't have to do dishes.

He heard voices coming from the saloon. Two Mexicans had stopped in for a drink. The owner dropped the tin plates in the dishpan and, wiping his hands on his shirt, he headed for the bar.

Bart was exhausted and decided to turn in. He checked on Buck before using the outhouse. As he climbed the ladder to the loft, he could hear the murmur of voices from the saloon. It sounded like a few more men had joined the first two.

* * *

The sun was just breaking the eastern horizon

when Bart stepped outside. In his hand he carried a cold cup of the prior night's coffee and over his shoulder his saddlebags. He had heard Wolfgang snoring in the far corner of the trading post.

Gulping down the last of the coffee, he set the cup on a log near the wood pile and went to get the buckskin. Leading it down to the Brazos River, he let it drink its fill. He then picketed it on some sun-baked grass. It was dry this summer, with rain being scant.

He put a pot of water on a small fire to heat and then stripped down. Retrieving a cake of brown soap from the saddlebags, he walked naked into the river for a much-needed bath. The cold water running over his body was refreshing.

Emerging with drops of water glistening on his well-muscled body, he shivered in the morning chill. He huddled over the fire while his body dried. Then, pulling on a clean pair of long johns, he got out his straight razor.

Finally shaved and dressed in his clean spare clothes, he led the buckskin back into the lean-to. He could hear the owner clanging with pans on the stove. Bart hoped the dollar a day included breakfast.

It did. Enjoying the last of his flapjacks covered with sorghum, Bart held a cup of coffee. Wolfgang had not been very talkative that morning. He was nursing a tequila hangover.

"Hey, Bart, if you take care of my horses, clean the stable, and sweep out the saloon, I'll give you a free night. My head is too heavy to do anything."

Without thinking, Bart nodded. "Be happy to."

It was mid-day when all the chores were done. Other than taking care of his horses, Wolfgang had neglected most of the cleaning. Bart washed his face and hands and went into the trading post. The owner was feeling much better. He had the three day-old beans warming on the stove.

"Come and get something to eat. One of the Mexicans brought a loaf of bread last night to trade for a couple drinks. It will go good with the beans."

Sitting down to the meal, Bart found that the beans had a bit of a bite to them from fermentation. The bread was excellent. The owner brought up the Dabney place again.

"One of the Mexicans told me that the place was still available. A lawyer in Waco is handling the sale. You can get the whole works for $400. They got some cows, but they ain't worth much. Maybe a couple horses. Buildings will need repair. You appear handy."

"Maybe I'll take the buckskin into Waco this afternoon and look up that lawyer," Bart said.

The ride into town was somber. He wondered if he would see Millie. Bart did not plan on going into the Mustang. He did not trust his temper if he found her with a customer, especially coming out of the back room. He rode slowly past the saloon, hoping she would step out. No such luck.

He saw a sign with 'Lawyer' written on it. An arrow pointed the way up a set of stairs to a small office. His knock on the door was answered by a thin, gray-haired man with wire rimmed spectacles. He squinted at Bart and motioned him to enter.

"The name's Hanson. What is it that I can do for you?" the lawyer asked.

"I'm interested in the Dabney place. Are you the fellow handling it for the Boston son?"

The lawyer slowly looked the big man, staring

at his worn, patched shirt and trousers. The weapons were impressive, but that did not mean the man in front of him had any money.

"They want . . . ah, $500 for it. You get some fine ranch buildings and an impressive herd," the small man said, rubbing his chin.

"I heard it was $400 and the buildings need work. Also know that beef are only worth what hides and tallow will bring," Bart countered. "Despite the poor quality of the place, I am ready to pay $300 in gold for it."

The lawyer Hanson closed the ledger in front of him a bit harder than necessary. "I have been given the task to secure a reasonable price for the ranch. I believe $500 is an excellent price."

Bart turned to leave. "Have you ridden to the place? If you had, I don't believe you could ask that much and sleep at night."

Once back on the street, he was in no hurry to go anywhere. The mercantile was just up the street and he had not gotten supplies. Walking along, dodging the road apples, he heard a team and buggy coming up behind him. He stepped aside quickly, the team barely missing him. In a cloud of dust, the buggy stopped.

Whirling around, Bart glowered at the driver. "Watch your damn driving, mister!"

Sitting tall in the seat was Axel Gerber. "You stay the hell out of the road, Nevell."

The short, white moustache of Axel was perfectly groomed. He wore a tailored wool suit and a beaver skin top hat.

"You going to a funeral, or wedding?" Bart inquired.

"I just got back from Fort Graham. Two of my

men were arrested for killing some soldiers. Was told you killed another," Axel snarled.

"He shot first. I was more accurate."

"You best keep out of the way of my boy Dieter. He has blood in his eye about you."

"You just keep him out of my way," Bart warned. "He is hot-headed and I don't want to kill him."

The rancher shifted uneasily in the carriage. "You hurt my boy and I'll come for you, Nevell. You may kill me, but I'll get lead into your ugly carcass."

With that, Axel slapped the horses with the end of the reins and sped away. Bart stared after him. He didn't envy the rancher raising a son like Dieter Gerber.

The mercantile was owned by Tom Cadwell. He smiled as Bart came in. "What can I do for you?"

Bart fumbled in his shirt pocket and brought out a list of goods he needed. "Can you fill this for me?"

Looking the list over, the man smiled. "I will have to cast some bullets for the Colt. Can have them ready for you tomorrow. Got the rest, though. You can take some now or get it all with the bullets."

"I'll stop by and get it tomorrow."

"Saw you in the Mustang yesterday. Whatever you said to Millie sure upset her. She was crying and finally had to leave work. She is a favorite, you know," the proprietor said.

Bart felt the muscles on his back tighten. He was half a thought away from dressing down the merchant. Fighting back the desire, he nodded. "Until tomorrow then, Mister Cadwell."

It was time to get back to Wolfgang's.

CHAPTER FIVE

Bart spent the evening drinking coffee and talking to Wolfgang's customers in the saloon. Some recognized him from his previous trip to the area and turned to leave. The owner called them back, assuring them that this wasn't the same man that they'd known before.

He learned a little more about the Dabney place. There were about 200 head of longhorns, maybe some horses. The ranch house had burnt, but the barn and bunk house were still there.

Learning about the house burning concerned Bart. He had hoped to bring Millie to the ranch. Without a proper home, it would be more difficult to encourage her.

Comments by the customers on the cleanliness of the saloon made Bart feel good. Wolfgang stood behind the bar, proud as ever. It had been a long time since the place had looked as good.

Bart slept restlessly that night. He was unsure of buying the Dabney place. He hadn't heard of another in the area available in his price range. He thought about Millie. Maybe she didn't feel about him like he did for her. Could he have misread the tenderness shown as she had nursed him back to health? He had also made an enemy of Dieter Gerber. If he had to kill the boy, he would also have to kill the father.

He respected the elder Gerber. The man had come into this part of Texas and carved out a ranch, fighting Indians, Mexicans, and the severe environment. He had been successful, and offered stability to the area.

Heading back toward Waco the next morning, his eyes were heavy from lack of sleep. The bright sun felt good on his back. He had decided to purchase a pack horse to carry the new supplies.

His first stop was at the livery stable. The hostler was busy cleaning the stalls, pitching the droppings and soiled bedding onto a wooden cart. A burro hitched to the cart stood patiently, waiting for the next command to move.

Waiting for the man to pitch the last couple forkfuls into the cart, he watched as the hostler gave the command, "Out." The obedient burro pulled the cart outside and around the stable.

"You've got to follow it out?" Bart asked.

"Nope, it'll stop near the pile and wait for me to come and empty the cart."

"The name's Bart Nevell. Want to talk to you about a packhorse."

"I remember you. The fellow I got the place from used to let you sleep off your drunks here. When he didn't have you cleaning the stalls, it was my job. I'm Junior Jones."

"Junior, after your pa?"

"Naw. My ma liked the sound of it and named me that."

"Now," Bart said, "about the packhorse. I'd like to look over your stock."

Junior led him to the corral on the end of the building. A half-dozen mustangs stood with their heads hanging, soaking up the sun. The hostler pointed at an older-looking horse. Bart noticed that two of Junior's fingers were missing. They were most likely lost while breaking horses.

Taking a rope off one of the posts, the hostler expertly dropped a loop over the chosen horse's neck. Even before the rope tightened, the mustang moved to the rail fence and stretched its nose out, anticipating a treat.

"I been kinda making a pet out of this one," the man said. He then rubbed the side of its head and scratched around its ears.

Bart walked back and forth, looking the animal over. It had good legs and a straight back. Mr. Jones showed him the teeth, which confirmed the age.

"I figure it's about 20 years-old. Lots of life left in this animal," Junior said, leading the horse to the pole gate.

"If this one is a pet, why are you willing to sell it?" Bart asked.

"It's too old for working cattle. I remember when you were here before. You would be tough as hob on other men, but always took good care of your horse."

Over the next half-hour the men talked horses and dickered over a price. When the deal was done, Bart had a sturdy packhorse and a rig to carry them.

Walking away with the buckskin and mustang in tow, Bart glanced back and saw Junior heading around the barn, where the burro waited patiently to have the cart emptied.

Bart called over his shoulder, "Hey, horse, this is Buck, you might want to teach him a thing or two about how to treat its rider." The mustang snorted softly as though answering yes.

He walked up the rutted street in the direction of Cadwell's place to pick up the supplies. Two boys ran by him rolling a hoop with sticks. Just beyond them Bart saw the building with the front porch lined with barrels, sacked goods, hand tools, and lamps.

Tying the horses at the rail in front of the mercantile, Bart strode in the door and came face to face with Dieter Gerber.

Crowded by the big man, Dieter was forced to step back. "I'm gonna kill you, Nevell," he snarled, standing with his hand hovering over his revolver.

Bart knew that he was at a disadvantage in close quarters. Bringing the Colt Dragoon up would be too slow. Dieter had a smaller Patterson and could get it into play much easier.

Stepping quickly toward the young man, Bart led with a solid right to the chest. Dieter stumbled back against the sales counter. He charged at Bart, sending them both crashing through the door, tumbling into the street alongside the startled horses.

Rolling and twisting in the dusty road, the two men looked for an advantage to get a finishing punch. With Dieter on top, Bart was taking several blows to the head and shoulders. Bracing himself, he pitched with his legs and sent Gerber head over heels into the dust.

Leaping onto his feet, Bart stood and circled the young man. Dieter had lost his revolver on the ground during the struggle. They exchanged punches, jabbing and deflecting blows.

Bart realized that he outweighed the younger man and had a longer reach. But this was the first fight he'd had in years when sober. Normally, anger mixed with alcohol drove him with a killing rage. Surprisingly, he found himself thinking about wearing down and disabling the man he was fighting with, rather than killing him. He was on unfamiliar ground on how to accomplish this.

A shout stopped the two men. "What the hell is going on here?"

It was Axel Gerber. Stopping momentarily, the two men looked at the older man.

"Dieter, get yourself back to the ranch right now." Red-faced with anger, Axel sent the boy away.

Bart, dusty and cut, stood looking at Axel. "He's a big boy. He can fight his own battles."

"I warned you, Nevell. You kill my boy, and I will come after you."

"You sending him home like that was worse than him taking a beating," Bart warned.

"I have seen you finish fights. Too often the result is a burial. It will not happen to my son."

Axel Gerber scooped up the boy's Patterson and strode quickly away. Watching him go, the big man shook his head and said to nobody in particular, "You should have let the fight finish. Now the damn kid will have to kill me."

Tom Cadwell stood in front of his damaged door with his hands on his hips. "Someone is going to pay for the door," he snapped.

"Put the damn thing on my bill," Bart said, as he carefully checked the cuts on his face.

"Well, come on in and I'll put something on those cuts." With that the owner turned, kicking the mangled door frame aside, and led the way inside.

The merchant had the bullets cast for the dragoon and the other supplies from the list in two sacks. He had figured the amount owed on a piece of packaging paper. Taking a stub of a pencil, he added the cost of repairing the door to the bottom.

Digging coins from his money belt, the bruiser paid the bill. Grabbing up the sacks, he turned to leave the mercantile. On the way out, he took a handful of crackers from a barrel, expecting a demand for additional payment. None came.

Bart was securing the supplies on the mustang when he saw the lawyer walking towards him. He felt tired from a poor night's sleep, and the young Dieter had delivered some bruising punches that were now starting to ache. The last thing he wanted to do is talk about the Dabney place.

Lawyer Hanson called out to him, "Mr. Nevell, I need to talk to you about the property."

Waving him away, Bart turned to mount the buckskin. "Not today, sir. I will be back another day to discuss the ranch."

"It is important we talk now." The lawyer stopped on the walk, noticing the broken door. Stepping around it, he stood at the edge of the walk, which brought him eye-to-eye with Bart.

"What is so important that it can't wait? You afraid I might find out that the ranch house burnt?" Bart asked.

This caused the lawyer to pause a moment. He

might not have known about the fire. "Oh my, no. I did receive a letter, just today, that authorizes me to lower the price. I could even go to $350."

"Thanks, but no thanks, Lawyer Hanson," Bart said, swinging into the saddle. Turning the horses, he started to leave.

Running alongside the horses, Hanson shouted, "Wait, wait, Mr. Nevell! It will cost me, but I will match your price."

By the time Bart left town that afternoon, he was the new owner of the Dabney Ranch.

CHAPTER SIX

Bart rode toward Wolfgang's feeling good about the price he paid for the ranch. At one point he almost turned around to go back and find Millie to let her know. He then thought the better of it, wanting to see the place first, hoping to describe it in such a way to convince her to join him.

Wolfgang smiled broadly as Bart told him about the purchase of the Dabney ranch. "You will make it ranch to be proud of, just like the Englishman did," the man told him.

"It is just a small place," Bart replied. "I will be lucky to scratch a living out of the 1,000 acres."

Reaching for a bottle of rye on the back bar, the owner said, "We must drink to your new home."

Bart almost agreed, and then shook his head. "I best not. I am hoping you have some of the items I will need. I only got traveling supplies at Cadwell's."

It was two days later before Bart rode into the barnyard leading the mustang, heavily loaded with supplies and gear. The property was a day's ride south of Waco.

The fireplace chimney stood as a monument above the charred remains of the ranch house. To his right was the low barn with a split pole corral. Across the yard stood the bunkhouse, with its door sagging. For the time being, it would serve as his home. Two other smaller buildings were burnt behind the bunkhouse.

A spring-fed brook ran behind the remains of the house. It gave the promise of good water and fresh trout. He stripped the gear from the horses and led them to the water for a drink. Bart scooped a cup full of water and grinned. "Nice and fresh, hey, Buck?"

Turning the horses loose in the corral, he noted that a couple of the posts were leaning, possibly snapped at ground level. He would make it a point to fix them before the animals discovered it and decided to go wandering.

Walking into the barn, he breathed deep of the earthy aroma. He found a fork and some hay that should still be good. He tossed a couple forkfuls over the corral rails for Buck and the mustang. Walking around the barn, he made mental notes of items that needed repair. He was pleased that the list was short.

The bunk house showed evidence that somebody had been staying there. It probably was a traveler passing through. He had been told that all cowhands had left shortly after the funeral. Mr. Dabney had died in the spring.

There was an open lean-to against the barn that had a forge, an anvil, and various tools. He found a hammer and shoeing nails. He used these to fix the leather hinge on the bunkhouse door. A little adjustment and it was opening and closing solidly.

After taking a mid-day break to eat, he spent the rest of the afternoon cleaning and repairing the buildings. There was a well near the bunkhouse. It was within easy distance of the watering trough. A bucket and wash basin sat on a flat boulder nearby.

The only surprise he found was a vegetable garden and a few acres of corn. Someone had been harvesting vegetables and weeding the garden. Whoever had been staying in the bunkhouse probably took advantage of the things planted before old man Dabney died. Maybe a couple of the guys lived within an easy ride. Bart noticed that any sign of their coming and going was missing.

"Well, the vegetables will be a welcome addition to beans and jerky." He then laughed, "Dang gum it, I ain't been here a full day and already I'm talking to myself."

After making supper on the stove in the bunkhouse, he saddled the mustang and decided to see how it handled. It snorted and nuzzled him while being saddled. He didn't remember another horse looking so forward to being ridden.

The mustang was surefooted and responded to the slightest command of the reins or knees. He rode a mile radius around the buildings. He saw several cows, many of the young stock unbranded. He was told there were horses, but there was no sign of them.

The grass was good, offering plenty of grazing for the animals. There was mesquite, and creosote bush. Along the brook grew scrub brush and juniper. He passed a scattering of hardwoods and conifers. There was a canyon that could be blocked off on both ends, making a simple holding area for roundup and branding.

Pleased with what he saw, Bart knew the price he paid for the land was a bargain. There were also another couple of sections that could be used for grazing. If the ranch did well, he could try to purchase more property.

It felt good to ride back into the ranch yard and call it his. Bart had never owned land before. He sat in front of the bunkhouse and planned the construction of the new ranch house. Finally tired, he turned to go into the building. Something slammed in the barn.

In the half-light of dusk, he first glanced at the corral. The buckskin was staring at the barn, while the mustang calmly chewed on the dried hay.

It could have been the wind slamming something, or a wild animal. Figuring he should check it out, Bart loosened the revolver in his holster and strode bravely to the barn.

"Damn it now, you are a grown man. A noise in the night should not scare you," he scolded himself. Truth was, sleeping in the open country didn't bother him at all. Yet around old buildings he was uncomfortable. Worrying about ghosts, maybe. That was unlikely because Bart did not believe in ghosts, but still there was something worrisome.

He entered the barn. He checked the empty horse stalls, around the hay pile, and the tack room. "Nothing," he muttered. Turning to leave the barn, he froze. Outlined in the doorway was a large, dark form. He grabbed for his gun.

"Don't shoot, massa, lordy, don't shoot me," the man begged.

With the gun half-drawn, Bart stopped. "Are you living in my barn?" All of a sudden, the garden and the evidence in the bunkhouse made sense.

The man backed out of the barn and stood in the fading light. "Yes, massa, I is."

Bart stood looking at the handsome, middle-aged black man who had lowered his head, afraid to make eye contact with the big man.

"What do they call you?" he asked.

"Joshua, massa, they calls me Joshua."

Bart noticed that the man was shaking. Why, he did not know, not realizing his size and normal scowl was a frightening thing in the daylight and much more so in the dusk.

Annoyed that this slave was hiding in his barn, and probably a runaway, he decided to just run him off.

"I want you to go. Leave here right now. This is my property and I haven't got room for you around here," Bart ordered.

"I can't, massa, this here is my home. I belongs to you, massa," Joshua pleaded.

That stopped Bart. This man belonged to him? He had seen lots of slaves in Texas, but had never thought too much about them other than if you needed something, you could holler at them to go get it and they would.

"I don't need a slave. Tomorrow, I'll write a note giving you your freedom and then you can go wherever you want," Bart informed the man.

"No, massa. I can't go," the black man said.

"Damn it now, if I say you can go, you can go. And for all that's holy, stop calling me massa. The name is Bart."

Shifting his feet and staring at the ground, the man replied, "I kin speak better. Massa Dabney learned us. But it ain't right to most folks. And you is my massa."

Frustrated, Bart snorted. "Damn you anyway. You ain't making any sense. Go back in the barn for now. We'll figure this out in the morning."

Leaving the man standing in front of the barn, he went into the bunkhouse, slamming the door behind him.

"Damn slaves weren't a part of this deal," he said, kicking a chair out of the way as he passed the table. Dropping his gun belt onto the floor, he sat heavily on a cot. He scratched his head, trying to clear his thinking. Sighing, he kicked off his boots and laid back, with one leg on the bed and the other hanging on the floor.

He kept thinking about the black man in his barn. The man must be a runaway. That would explain why he couldn't leave. Bart didn't have papers on him, so he couldn't give him his freedom. If grabbed by slave hunters, the man would be returned to his owner and probably beaten, or worse.

Bart's thoughts drifted back to his youth. His father had owned slaves to work the small, poor plantation in South Carolina. He'd drank too much and had been mean when drunk. There had been many whippings of slaves. If one had moved too slowly, or had done something incorrectly, or had just been in the wrong place when his father was ranting, punishment had been swift and severe.

Even Bart and his younger brother, Samuel, had not been safe around the drunken father. Their mother had died when Bart was 15. Before her death, she had always done her best to protect her boys. After that, hardly a week went by without several cutting strokes from the riding crop carried by the violent patriarch.

When Bart was 16, he had heard the screams of a girl coming from one of the slaves' quarters. He had run to find out what was wrong and had found his father raping and beating a young black girl. Without thinking, Bart had grabbed a discarded shovel handle and hit his father. Consumed by rage from all of the abuse he had received, he had kept striking the man until he lay unconscious and bleeding on the dirt floor of the shack.

Whether or not he had killed his father, Bart did not know. With nothing but the clothes on his back, he had left the plantation and traveled west. Being large for his age, he had joined the army and spent four years fighting and relocating Cherokee, due to the Act of 1830.

Once out of the army, Bart had used the experience he had gained scouting or guiding hunting parties. Never had he attempted to establish a new home, nor look back to the home he had ran from.

Now he laid on the cot, with the unpleasant memories of his youth flooding back. For years, drink had been his escape from the past. That, and the rage he often felt, were traits passed on by his father.

Bart knew all too well that slaves were just property. Your property to use, abuse, or discard as you saw fit. They had value, if sold. Or you could work them to death and, if you had the money, replace them. They had no right to complain or to have free will.

Tossing and turning, Bart tried to shut off his mind. His father's angry face kept appearing as he began to doze, bringing him wide awake. If ever he wanted a drink to shut out the past, it was now. Seeing the man in the barn had opened a very deep wound.

Finally exhausted, he slept. It was full light when he awoke, sun streaming in the window, reflecting on the dust particles rising off the floor. He had worked hard the day before and had not cleaned up.

Stripping off his sour shirt, he walked over to the well and pulled up a bucket of water. Filling the basin, he washed. Using a threadbare towel he had found, he dried himself. Bart put on his clean shirt and combed back his hair with his fingers.

It was time to face up to his past and the man in the barn. Taking a moment, he checked on the horses first. They had already been fed and watered. In the dust he saw the boot prints of the man he had met, as well as smaller barefoot prints.

Walking into the barn he found the black man sitting on a small, three-legged stool. He stood up quickly when he saw Bart.

"Ah done took care of da hosses, massa."

"I noticed. Where are the others?" Bart asked.

"Others, massa?" Joshua replied.

"First off, I want you to quit calling me master. If you got to call me something, call me boss, or mister. And yes, I saw the footprints. Where are the others?" Bart asked again, staring sternly at the man.

Unsure of what to do, Joshua's chin started to quiver. It was something Bart had often seen as a youngster. It made him feel sick inside.

"Damn, man, you are not in trouble. I need to know how many others there are, so I can figure out what to do," Bart said, fighting to keep the sound of anger out of his voice.

Turning, Joshua went to the back of the barn

and pulled open a trapdoor on the floor. He motioned to whoever was in there to come out. Bart watched as three more slaves emerged: A woman, a young boy and a girl.

"Massa, . . . ah, Boss Bart, this here is my wife, Sara, and chillin, Nathaniel and Mary."

Bart noted a bit of pride showing as Joshua introduced his family.

"Where did you come from?" Bart asked. Joshua looked confused. "Where did you run away from?"

"We is from here, Boss Bart. Massa Dabney owned us and three others. Hunters came after the massa died and caught the others. We hid in the old root cellar below the house. It were used til da water done gone over and filled it. Them hunters burnt da house right over our heads. We got out da back hatch and hid in da new cellar here in da barn."

"So, these hunters tried to burn you out of the house and didn't know there was another way out of the old cellar?"

Nodding, Joshua added, "Yes, Boss Bart, da old cellar hatch had brush growed agin it. Da flood had ruin it. They didn't know of da new one in the barn. They watch and hunt many days. We hid and only come out in da dark. We feared you was a hunter."

"Well, you were lucky the brook had ruined the old cellar. It that hadn't happened, you would not have had the new cellar to hide in," Bart agreed.

Looking at the fearful group, he continued. "We have a problem. I don't have paper on you, so anyone can come here and claim you are runaways. I would have no choice but to let them take you."

Joshua stepped forward with his eyes to the ground, and handed Bart rolled-up sheets of paper. Unrolling them, he saw that they were Charles Dabney's ownership papers of the slaves. Also in them was a document giving Joshua's family freedom after his death.

"This says you are a free man. You can go anywhere. Why haven't you left? This here would protect you from slave hunters," Bart pointed out.

"When we hid, da others show da paper to hunters. They laugh and burn paper. Then take them away to sell," Joshua said with emotion, forgetting his place for a moment and looking Bart square in the eye.

Turning, the big man took a deep breath. "I will take you and your family to Waco and make sure they know you are free. You can then make your way to the north and a safer place."

"Boss Bart, this here is da only home we know. If'n you send us away, some hunters will take us away, jess like da others. Here with you is da only safe place."

Frustrated, Bart kicked the dirt and walked over to the corral. The mustang came up to him and nudged him with its nose. "You're a good horse. I got a problem here. I got a family here with me that is afraid to leave. If sent away, I'm sure they would be captured and sold. I can use the help on the ranch, but made myself a promise years ago never to own another man."

The horse snorted and shoved Bart. "Even you don't want to hear about my problems." Slapping the horse on the shoulder and sending it running around the corral, Bart walked back to the family.

"Joshua, here is how I see it. First, these papers say you are free, so when we talk, you can look at me.

Second, I can use the help around here. I will pay you for work done. If at some point you want to leave, tell me and go. I am guessing the burnt buildings behind the bunkhouse were yours and the others who were taken away. You can set up housekeeping in part of the bunkhouse."

Without waiting for an answer, Bart walked away to make himself some breakfast. It felt like a weight had been taken off his shoulders.

As he stoked up the coals in the bunkhouse stove, he heard soft footsteps coming up from behind. Turning, he looked down at Sara.

"I want to thank you, Boss Bart. Joshua has been hiding us and watching for the hunters for some time now. Until you came, we didn't see any way out of our problem. You have given us back our life."

"You speak well," he said. "I am not giving you anything. Joshua will work, and in return get paid. If you want to work, I will pay you."

"Thank you, I would like to help. Boss Bart, Joshua speaks well also, but he had found if he speaks above his place, it brings him and us trouble."

"Well, you tell him that when he speaks to me, I want him to talk so I can understand him. With others, he can talk anyway he sees fit."

CHAPTER SEVEN

The following days were work, and more work. The first thing that needed to be done was setting up housekeeping. A wall was put up in the bunkhouse, dividing it into two rooms. Another door was put in, giving Joshua's family a private entrance.

Sara took over the cooking, cleaning and laundry. The children were seven and nine years-old. They were too young to work the ranch, but their mother found plenty of chores for them, including taking care of the garden.

Joshua took a liking to the mustang and rode it whenever possible. Bart knew more horses would be needed to work the ranch. They were pushing the longhorns toward the canyon for counting and branding when they took a break for something to eat.

Bart sat looking at the grazing cattle. "We need more horses. Tomorrow I will go into Waco and see what is available. I won't be able to afford the best stock, but if we continue on with just these two horses, they'll be ruined."

Joshua sat scratching designs in the dust with a stick. Tossing it aside, he looked at Bart. "You have horses, boss. Master Dabney had me drive them to a friend's ranch in a valley two days' ride south. He was afraid men would steal them while he was sick."

"You're telling me I own some horses I don't know about?"

"Yes, boss, there were twelve. Some might've been lost or taken by the Kitsai or Hueco."

"Well, Joshua, we best get on over to the valley and bring them back. We'll leave early in the morning."

The two-day trip was mostly through marshland. They were traveling somewhat parallel to the Brazos River. The town of Austin was further west, another place Bart remembered little of. He had been drunk for a week when there.

The valley ranch was owned by a fellow Englishman and friend of Charles Dabney. Henry Collins had a ranch of several thousand acres. The valley itself would take days to ride across.

The wiry, white-haired Englishman knew Joshua well. He immediately sent some of his vaqueros out to bring in the horses. "Bloody good horsemen the Spanish are. I was about to have dinner. Join me, please. Your man Joshua knows his way around here and will tend to the horses when they are brought back. You can sleep in the guest room."

Bart followed Henry into the large, Spanish-style ranch house. The man was proud of the fine things he owned and spoke of several of them as he showed his guest to the dining room. The large table was set with fine crystal and silver. The ornate, straight-backed chairs looked barely strong enough to hold the big man. Bart sat carefully on the one he was directed to.

He realized that had he ridden up as a ranch hand to get the horses, he would have been directed to eat with the other cowboys and sleep in the bunkhouse. As a fellow land owner, he was viewed and treated much differently. He was unsure if it felt good or not.

The food was served by black servants, more than likely slaves owned by Mr. Collins. The meal was pheasant and small new potatoes dripping with butter. Also, a vegetable which Bart did not recognize, but did enjoy.

The dinner conversation was mostly about the weather, grass conditions, and the price of horses. The Collins ranch also had a fair number of sheep, and the wool was exported out of the port of Galveston.

Brandy was offered after the meal, but Bart declined. He was already having a hard enough time maneuvering around the fancy house without the drink. He did enjoy an excellent cigar.

When it was time to go to bed, Bart was thankful to finally be alone. The Englishman's guest bed was short, with a head and foot board. He had to lay diagonal to straighten out. Still, his feet hung off. The soft mattress and down-filled pillows almost made him feel like he was being smothered.

Breakfast was a simple affair in the courtyard of the house. The choice was tea or a very strong coffee mixed with milk and sugar. Henry talked about the number of head he owned and how many men worked for him. The conversation flowed into Texas politics and problems with Mexico.

Bart was never happier than when they finished eating and headed for the corral to look over the horses. He decided that being a good guest was much harder than being a good host. He could not wait to be on his way.

The horses were in better shape than he had hoped. They were mostly mustangs. There was also a large sorrel and a pinto. He noticed a small gray mare. If Millie ever joined him, it would be a perfect horse for her.

All twelve were found. Joshua sat on the fence, his face beaming as he watched the horses. "Da hosses will be okay for da ranch. Ours are saddled, Boss Bart."

"Thanks, Joshua. I will just be a minute. I need to check what we owe Mr. Collins."

Henry was busy directing his vaqueros on what needed to be done. He turned and smiled as Bart walked up. "Find the stock in good shape?"

"That we did, Henry. What do I owe you for holding the horses for me?"

"Charles Dabney was a good man and friend. You are keeping the CD brand going. You owe me nothing, my good man. Stop by again, I enjoyed the company."

Within the hour, Bart and Joshua were off with the horses. The animals moved on easily and required little herding. The two men rode in the back or to one side to keep out of the dust.

"I notice you switch your style of speaking, depending on who you're talking to," Bart said.

"Well, boss, a person like me can't take chances. If we use what Master Dabney called the king's English, we would be punished for trying to be above our place. Master Dabney taught Sara and me to read and write. We even learned our numbers. If others knew this it would bring us and you much trouble."

Bart rode quietly, remembering. What Joshua said was true. He had seen much of what the black man had said when growing up in the Carolinas. He knew that he couldn't change the way things were, but on his small ranch, proper speech and learning would be okay.

The sun was just above the horizon when the two men stopped near a babbling brook for the evening. They strung a picket line and managed to get all the horses tied for the night. Ducks flew low above them heading for the marsh just east of their camp.

Both men had been treated well by Henry Collins and had had a good breakfast, and cheese sandwiches to be eaten mid-day. It was dark when Bart started a fire and put on some coffee. "I believe I will make due with just the coffee. Help yourself to whatever you'd like, Joshua."

"I saved part of my sandwich and that will do me fine, Boss Bart."

"In the morning we can put our saddles on a couple of the new horses," Bart suggested. "Our buckskin and mustang are just about played out."

Tired from the day in the saddle, the men rolled out their blankets and turned in after a cup of coffee. The half-pot remaining would be re-warmed in the morning. Bart was feeling good about the stock they'd picked up at the Collins ranch. Five were mares and would make good breeding animals, the rest were geldings.

They were lulled to sleep by the chorus of the cicadas and coyotes on the hunt. Cloud cover moved in overnight, accompanied by oppressive humidity. Bart kicked off his blanket at first light, his clothes damp from sweat. Joshua was already awake and leading the horses to water. He had put tinder on last night's ashes and the remaining coals had started it smoldering.

Shaking out his boots before putting them on, Bart said, "Now this is the kind of weather I remember in Texas. The air is so heavy, a man could use his knife to cut out a chunk and fill the coffeepot."

"It sure is damp, Boss Bart," Joshua agreed. "I thick it's fixing to rain."

"Well, we best grab a quick bite and head for the ranch," the big man said. "Looks like the weathers coming from the southeast and maybe we can stay ahead of it for a while."

Joshua chose one of the new mustangs with a white blaze on its forehead to ride. Bart chose the pinto. Once mounted the mustang began to crow hop, arching its back and landing stiff-legged as it resisted being ridden. Joshua stuck to the animal while it worked out the kinks. Soon he had it standing quietly.

Watching the black handle the unruly horse, Bart was pleased with how well Joshua rode the animal. "If any of the other horses need taming down, you got the job."

The rain caught up with them about mid-morning. The men donned their slickers, which kept the drops off them but were hot and clammy to wear, leaving their clothing damp from sweat. Both of the horses had been used to drive cattle and were quick to respond to any of the driven horses that tried to stray.

It was still drizzling when they reached the ranch. Both men had taken off the slickers and let the precipitation cool them. They brought the animals past the stream so they could drink before driving them into the ranch yard. Nathaniel had the corral open, and in short order the horses were stomping and snorting as they circled inside the corral, happy to be back at the ranch.

While Bart and Joshua stripped the gear from their horses, the young black brought out forkfuls of hay and pitched them into the feeding racks. "Your boy will be a great help with the horses," Bart said, observing Nathaniel.

"For his age, he is a fair rider also," Joshua proudly replied.

The pinto and blazed mustang were turned loose in the corral. Bart carried his saddle into the barn and put it onto the side wall of one of the stalls. Once it dried a bit, he planned to come out and clean it with saddle soap. Joshua had brought his saddle into the tack room and then headed for their side of the bunkhouse.

Bart stood in the open bay of the barn and thought about plans for the ranch. Everything he thought about included Millie. As soon as the roundup was completed he needed to start re-building the house. The chimney and fireplace could be re-used. The original house may have had three or four rooms. He would start with two. The front would be a kitchen and large sitting room.

As he headed for his side of the bunkhouse, Bart was pleased that the rain had stopped. The sky was clearing to the east, promising good weather tomorrow. He and Joshua could continue rounding up the cattle for branding and castration as needed.

Reaching the bunkhouse, Bart began to pull off his wet clothing. "Leave the damp stuff near the door. I will be doing a wash tomorrow." It was Sara, and she was bringing him a heaping plate of greens and rabbit for his supper.

The next morning, Bart fired up the forge. The horses they had brought from the Collins ranch needed to be shoed. He found everything he would need on the shelves in the lean-to. Joshua went to the corral and tossed a loop over the head of one of the new horses and led it to the lean-to.

By the end of the day the horses were shoed and all of them were tested under the saddle. Again, Bart was pleased with his purchase of the ranch. Tomorrow he and Joshua would push some more cattle in from the thickets and drifts that they had taken refuge in. The decision was made to keep the CD brand. On the next trip to Waco Bart would register it in his name.

While the air remained humid, the days were sunny. At the end of the week, Bart decided to ride into town. Joshua could keep an eye on the cattle that were already rounded up. So far, they estimated that there were over 100 in the herd. Bart hoped to double that by the time they were done.

Sara and the children had been busy tending a corn crop. In the coming years, Bart wanted to look into planting beans or even cotton. The price of beef was poor due to the long distance to market. If Bart was to drive the cattle to Galveston, they could be taken by ship to the Caribbean islands.

As Bart rode the buckskin towards Waco while leading two packhorses, he pondered what course of action would be best. He arrived in town early afternoon on the second day. As he rode down the street, the only thing on his mind was Millie. Hoping to catch sight of her on the street, he got the brand registered and placed his order at the mercantile. Tom Cadwell told him it would be a bit, so Bart went to the Mustang Saloon to get a bite to eat and hoped to see Millie.

A small spread of bread and cheese was at the end of the bar for those who were drinking. Bart walked into the dim establishment and ordered a beer. A couple men were at a table playing cards and one man towards the back was slumped over a table, sleeping.

Millie was nowhere to be seen. Bart knew it was early for the working girls to be at the saloon, but he did hope she'd be there. Making himself a sandwich of the bread and cheese that had been out for some time, Bart moved to a table and sat facing the door.

After an hour, he decided that he best be going if he was going to get the supplies and ride to Wolfgang's. Just before standing, there was the sound of ladies' laughter coming from outside. The batwings were pushed open and Millie and another lady walked in. For just a moment, Bart felt like a child caught with his hand in a cookie jar and sat, unsure of what to say.

As she noticed him, Millie broke into a broad smile and said, "Look who finally came in from the ranch."

Before he could respond, she bid her friend goodbye and joined the big man at his table. "Buy a girl a drink?" she asked.

"It's good to see you Millie," Bart replied. He signaled Tony, the bartender, to bring her a drink. "I was just about to give up seeing you."

"Well, you know I don't start until late," she said, accepting the drink from the bartender. "There is no money to be made before the cowboys come in."

"I am getting the ranch ready for the day you join me, Millie," he said, toying with his empty beer mug.

Shaking her head, she said, "I told you before that I am not cut out for living out on a ranch."

"Let me buy you another drink," he said as he enjoyed the sweet smell of the blond woman.

She stood up and gave him a peck on his whisker-covered cheek. "You best save your money for the ranch. It was nice seeing you again." With that she disappeared into the back room to get ready for the evening's work.

Feeling numb, Bart tossed a coin onto the bar to settle up for his beer and her drink. When he got to Cadwell's his supplies were ready. "You should get yourself a wagon," the owner said. "You'll need it to put in your winter supplies."

"Got me a wagon on the ranch," Bart replied. "A little bit of repair and it will be good as new."

Bart rode slowly past the Mustang, hoping to catch another glimpse of Millie. From inside came the sounds of the evening customers and the laughter of the women working them. "I won't give up," he mumbled.

It was dark when Bart arrived at Wolfgang's. He pulled the packs and gear off the horses and stowed them in the sagging barn. Using a sack, he rubbed the animals down before putting them into the stalls and giving them hay.

It was a good night for Wolfgang. Over a dozen customers were drinking and playing cards. The owner waved to Bart and brought him over a beer. "I got some stew made with a raccoon that was getting into my garden. I will bring you a bowl as soon as I finish serving some drinks."

All the tables were occupied, so Bart remained leaning against the bar, sipping the beer. The stew was made with some kind of peppers, giving it a bite. Brooding over Millie, the big man ignored the men around him. As he was eating the last spoonful of stew, the man next to him bumped his elbow sending the food across Bart's shirt.

Stepping away, Bart scowled at the man. "Careful, mister."

"I am sorry, señor," the tipsy Mexican replied. "I buy you a drink."

The man pushed a bottle of rye toward Bart. Shoving it back, Bart said, "I don't want your damn drink."

"You too good to drink with me?" the drunken Mexican challenged Bart.

Anger flashed through the big man. It hadn't been a good day so far, and this was not helping. Bart turned to face the man just in time to catch a ham-sized fist across his jaw. Dazed and stumbling backward, he was rushed by the Mexican. Bart came up against the wall as the man collided with him, pummeling the big man's midsection with punches.

A black rage soared through Bart that he hadn't felt since his last drunk. Oblivious to the punches, Bart braced himself against the wall and shoved the man away, following him to the floor as the man tripped. Pinning the man down, Bart began to beat him. Suddenly the big man saw stars and everything went dark.

It was night when Bart woke, lying on some bags of grain in Wolfgang's back room. He could hear the sounds of someone humming as they cleaned up the saloon. Slowly he sat up, his head aching. There was a good-sized lump on the back of his skull. His fists were badly scraped and it hurt to open and close his hands.

All of a sudden, the curtain covering the doorway was pulled aside. The lamp light from inside the saloon caused him to blink. "I see you are awake." The voice was Wolfgang's.

Groaning, Bart replied, "What the hell happened?"

"You were trying to kill one of my good customers and I had to hit you over the head," the owner told him.

"Well, I sure as hell didn't start it," Bart said, defending himself.

"Come on out," Wolfgang said. "I got a pot of coffee on."

* * *

The next morning Bart headed back toward his ranch. He had several bruises and ached all over. It had been some time since his last fight with Dieter and only the second fight being sober. Despite the results of the fight, Bart was feeling better. Thanks to the drunken customer, the big man had been given a chance to work off some of his frustrations.

An hour from Wolfgang's, Bart passed a small line shack. Grinning, he told his horse, "I might have to sleep here on my trips to Waco from now on. I may have me a bunch of mad Mexicans back at Wolfgang's."

The sight of the blackened chimney and the barn roof as he approached the ranch building gave him a feeling he was coming home. It was a feeling he had not had in a long time. What he faced in the future was lots of work, but he was looking forward to it.

The days flowed into weeks as Bart and Joshua's family worked the ranch. A tally of the cattle was taken. There were over 200 longhorns, with several being young and ideal for herd building. The job of branding the cattle was hot and dirty work for the two men. Sara made sure they were well-fed in the evening and the children would carry water to the branding area for Bart and Joshua.

Bart continued to take trips to Waco for supplies. Despite the fight, he would spend a night at Wolfgang's. Fortunately, he didn't run into the man he had fought with. Twice, he had met Millie. He would bring her up-to-date on what was being done on the ranch. Each time he had asked her to join him. While she no longer flatly said she wouldn't, he never left with a great amount of hope.

It was late August, and he needed to put in winter supplies. He also had extra corn he could sell. The wagon had been fixed and a team of mustangs were used to pull it. He headed toward Waco with bags of corn to sell. The two horses stepped lively in the cool morning air. Nate and Mary ran alongside, reminding him to bring them some peppermint sticks.

Promising to do so, he watched as they turned back, laughing and playing tag as they went. He felt a pang of regret. A man needed a wife and children. He feared he had missed his chance. Watching Joshua and Sara was probably the closest he would get.

The streets of Waco were busy. Several wagons with supplies stood filled and ready to go. Both the livery and Cadwell Mercantile had shown an interest in buying corn. Tom Cadwell's price was a bit higher, so that was Bart's destination.

He noticed a rugged-looking character standing in front of the saloon. The man had a drooping mustache and dark, cold eyes. He carried both a revolver and knife on his hips, and in his gloved hand was a bullwhip.

Bart felt like the man paid too much attention to him as he went by. Shaking off his uneasiness, he continued to the mercantile. Pleased with the price he received for the corn, he decided to purchase Joshua a revolver. Tom Cadwell had a Colt Paterson of the older style that was in good condition. After a little dickering, he added the gun and a spare cylinder to the list of supplies.

Joshua had an older rifle that had been Charles Dabney's, which was carried in a saddle scabbard, but when working cattle a rifle took too much time to get into action in the event trouble arose.

Bart left the store feeling good that he had money left after purchasing the supplies. He was looking at the revolver and checking its action as he walked up to the wagon.

"You planning on shooting me with that thing?" Looking up, his eyes met the clear, beautiful eyes of Millie. She sat with her bags on the wagon.

The big man's heart skipped a beat as he caught his breath. Without a word he put the revolver in with the rest of the supplies and climbed on the wagon, sitting next to Millie. Slapping the reins on the rumps of the team, he moved them out.

"Nothing to say, Bart Nevell?" she teased.

"You're being here has left me speechless. I never expected this to happen." His normal scowl softened to a crooked smile.

"I am not going with you to get married. I have decided that I want to be with you, and help you on the ranch. I have loved you a long time," she said.

He was out of place with this woman. Bart had never had the knack of knowing how to woo a lady. When he was drunk it had seemed easy, probably because it was just a transaction, not a relationship.

"I thank you for coming with me. I hope you change your mind and we get married someday." He quit talking, not trusting his voice.

He would have normally spent a night at Wolfgang's before heading for the ranch. Having Millie with him made him change his plans. Instead, they rode for the ranch. They would travel as far as the line shack. They could spend the night there and reach the ranch by mid-day.

With supper over, the two of them sat in the line shack. Millie cleaned up the dishes while Bart replaced the firewood and checked on the wagon and teams. He came back into the small building and saw Millie had pushed two cots together and made up the bed.

Bart sat at the table and fumbled with adjusting the lantern. Millie looked at him and stood with her hands on her hips. "Bart Nevell, don't sit there like a school boy. We aren't strangers to the night."

* * *

The wind was blowing softly, rustling the oak leaves next to the line shack. The big man was whistling while he hitched the team. The western sky was building thunderheads, giving the promise of rain before day's end.

Millie stepped out the door and shaded her eyes from the morning light. "Everything's finished in here. We can leave when you're ready."

She was wearing a simple dress, and Bart could see her supple figure as the wind ruffled the fabric. He paused a moment, thinking about the night before. Sleeping on cots was damned inconvenient. He would build a double bed as soon as they got back to the ranch.

With the wagon ready, he helped Millie get into the wagon. He still could not believe she was here with him. Normally a quiet man, Bart talked throughout the rest of the trip. He told her about his dream of growing the ranch. While he had mostly longhorns right now, he wanted to switch to horses. A good horse brought more money than the biggest cow.

The first thing Millie saw was the chimney of the burnt ranch house. Shortly after, the barn came in view. Bart was pointing out various landmarks when he stopped. A horse was tied at the corral. The paint was familiar, but he couldn't remember where he had seen it.

Concern began to build. Normally, the youngsters would come running to meet the wagon, especially with the prospect of getting a sweet. He could hear the sound of a hammer on iron coming from the tool room.

Stopping the wagon short of the barn, he asked Millie to wait. Moving quietly along the back of the building, he could hear weeping. Again, the hammering started. Stopping at the corner for a moment, he drew the Dragoon. Stepping around, he could see into the room. Anger surged through his veins. The man he had seen in front of the saloon was putting leg irons on Joshua and Sara.

"What in the hell do you think you are doing?" he shouted.

The man jumped and faced Bart with the uncoiled whip in one hand and the hammer in the other. "I am taking these runaways back for the reward. If you try and stop me, I'll have the law after you."

Bart could see the frightened faces of Nate and Mary sitting behind their parents. He wanted to kill this man in the worst way, but did not want to do it in front of the children.

"They are not runaways. Charles Dabney had paper on them and then freed them upon his death," Bart snarled.

The man snorted, "Let me see them."

"Like the last ones shown you. A little fire and they become runaways. Now you get the hell off my property," Bart ordered.

The movement of the man's arm was hardly noticeable. As though alive, the whip snaked out, wrapping around and cutting into the big man's arm. His Colt Dragoon fell to the ground.

Almost as a reflex while the lash burned in the flesh, Bart grabbed the whip and pulled as hard as his muscle-packed body could pull. Drawn off balance, the slave hunter fell forward towards Bart. He was met with a massive fist at the point of his jaw.

He fell like a poleaxed steer. Standing over the man, Bart fought with every fiber of his being, to not continue striking the man until he was a lifeless mass of cuts and bruises.

Joshua and Sara stood in stunned silence,

staring at the man lying unconscious on the ground. Bart picked up his revolver and slipped it into his holster. Then taking the hammer, he quickly removed the leg irons.

"Take the children and go to the bunkhouse. I will get rid of this man," he instructed them.

He loaded the man over the saddle, and tied his arms and legs under the horse's belly. He then led the animal well beyond the wagon and sent it galloping with a slap on the rump with the handle of the whip.

Walking back, Bart climbed into the wagon with Millie and drove it to the bunkhouse.

"Who was that man, Bart?" she asked.

"He hunts runaway slaves. Only in his case, it doesn't matter if you are a runaway or not. He can always find a buyer for any he catches," he said.

"I had seen him before around Waco. Thank god I never met him."

Yes, thank god, he thought.

CHAPTER EIGHT

The scare from the slave hunter was soon forgotten. The supplies were put away and the children smiled from ear to ear when they got the peppermint sticks. Bart was pleased to see Millie and Sara talking and laughing. The only mood that had not improved was that of Joshua. He was quiet, and his face remained strained.

"Joshua, come here," Bart requested. He reached into the wagon and brought out the Colt Paterson. "This here is the older caliber .28, but still a good weapon. A friend of mine had one like this and it shot quite well. Practice, keep it with you, and if a man like the hunter comes, shoot to kill."

The black man reached for the weapon, his hand shaking slightly. "Boss Bart, I shot a long gun a bit, but never the short one. If I kill a white man, they'll hang me quick."

"And if you don't, you're dragged off to work for a cruel man. Which one is better?" he said.

Awkwardly, Joshua strapped on the gun and

holster. It hung loose on his slim body. "Thank you, Boss Bart, I will poke another hole in the belt." Taking it back off, he carried it into the bunkhouse.

Walking into his side of the building, he saw Millie busy putting supplies away. Looking over her shoulder, she smiled. "You best get started on that double bed. We don't want any more falling through the crack of the cots."

There was plenty of work for everyone on the ranch. Bart had seen a good stand of grass not far from the barn. He and Joshua started cutting it with big sweeps of a scythe. Once dry, it was piled in stacks next to the barn. Nate and Mary loved sitting on top of the wagon load of hay, riding from the field to the barn.

Once the hay was cut, there was the last of the corn to harvest. For this a sickle was used for cutting the stocks. They were then bundled, to keep them off the ground and allow additional drying before removing the kernels from the cobs.

What Bart enjoyed most were the daily rides around the property to check on the stock. The longhorns had been moved further from the ranch to take advantage of grazing. This left the closer feed for colder winter weather.

This area of Texas did not get a lot of snow, but it could be cold and miserable during January and February. It was best during these times to keep your stock close. It made watching for predators easier.

He and Millie spent hours talking about the future. Bart had gotten her to agree to marry him in the spring. She insisted on going to a town away from Waco, a place where neither one was known.

They had a surprise visit from Henry Collins.

He was bringing a load of processed wool to the mercantile in Waco. He had six hens and a rooster with him.

"I thought you might like to have fresh eggs in the morning" Henry said, smiling.

"Thank you, that we will," Bart said. "It is a bit tight here, but we would be pleased if you spent the night."

Glancing around, he shook his head. "Your offer is appreciated, my friend, but I am expected in Waco. Another time, though."

Even though it was unspoken, Bart knew that their spartan accommodations were not up to his standards. With a hardy handshake, the Englishman climbed back onto his wagon. The black man driving the wagon flipped the reins to get the team moving. Turning, Henry Collins gave them a big wave as the wagon moved away.

That evening as they lay in bed, Bart commented on how nice it would be to have eggs for breakfast.

Millie snuggled up next to him. "First thing I will do is put a couple hens sitting on a nest. By spring the chicks will be grown and we can have fried chicken."

Running his fingers through her hair, Bart chuckled. "Maybe it can be for our wedding dinner."

"Just maybe," she said.

* * *

The gray mare turned out to be the perfect horse for Millie. She and Bart took several rides looking over the property. They had a stand of pine not far from the ranch. While sitting on one of the fallen logs, they planned their house.

"We can get plenty of long timbers from this growth and build a three, maybe four bedroom house," Bart said.

"Is that for all the kids you think we are going to have?" she teased.

"Truth is, I never figured on having children. It would be nice." Pulling her a little closer, he said, "Maybe with a fine house Henry Collins will even spend the night."

"Don't you worry about the neighbors. I think we have the best home in Texas."

While they chatted, Bart noticed two riders coming toward the barn. Squinting, he tried to figure out if he knew them.

"We best go on down and see what they want," he told Millie.

He held her horse while she climbed into the saddle. He liked to watch her graceful movements.

Swinging up on Buck, they trotted down to meet the rider. As they approached, Millie said she wanted to get back to the bunkhouse. Turning the gray, she rode off, her hair flowing in the wind.

Coming up to the men, Bart asked, "What can I do for you gents?"

The two were men were barely twenty and had the look of cowhands. "Was that Millie?" the taller one asked.

"Yes it was," Bart said. "If you're looking for work, I am afraid, we're not hiring."

The shorter cowboy, supporting a scraggly beard, smiled. "We heard someone had bought the old Dabney place. We had hoped for some fall work."

"My herd is small and the hay is made. Gerber may be hiring. He lost some hands this year."

Tilting his hat back, the tall one looked after Millie riding away. "Sure could use a cup of coffee. Mind if we come in and set a spell?"

"You got a long ride back to Waco, boys," Bart said, feeling a bit irritated. "I recommend you get started."

Pulling their horses around, the shorter one said, "If you have work come up, just ask for Lonnie or Ted when in Waco." They spurred their horses to a gallop, leaving the big man listening to their laughter.

Bart rode toward the barn. He knew this kind of behavior could be expected. Millie had been in Waco a long time and had known many men. He promised himself that no matter what, he would never react to any comment when she was with him. He also knew that the two of them would probably never be able to enjoy walking the streets of Waco.

After putting up the horses, Bart stopped by the bunkhouse to check on Millie. She smiled quickly when she saw him. "I'm going to bake some bread. If you get us a cow someday, we can have fresh bread with butter."

"That sounds mighty fine," he said. She sure knew how to lift the moment.

"And if you could, fetch me an armload of wood."

A cool October breeze was whipping up. Bart split enough to fill the woodbox. He then looked over the old house site. All of the charred remains had been cleared away. All that remained was the stone foundation and the fireplace. They had talked of building the house after the spring roundup and planting were done. With the fall work done, he decided that it was time to start building.

Measuring up the foundation, he decided to build to the original size first. It would make two bedrooms, a good size sitting room and kitchen. They had a ten-plate stove in the bunkhouse. This could be put in the middle of the large room for heat.

He checked over the fireplace. Other than some external scorching, it was in good order. It was fitted with a sturdy lug pole for hanging large pots. They were going to fill in the root cellar until Joshua reminded him of how well it had worked for them to escape the slave hunter.

Harnessing the team, he drove them up to the stand of pine. Tying the team off on the log, he and Millie had enjoyed this morning. Bart took the sharp, two-bit axe and began to fell trees. Taking large, accurate swings, he sent big chips flying. In less than an hour he had six trees down and limbed.

Deciding to cut them to length once he had them at the building site, he secured a log to the team using a length of stout rope, then skidded them one at a time down to the foundation. He repeated the cutting and skidding twice more before he heard Millie calling him to supper.

Stopping by the well, he washed his face and hands. The cool wind made the sweat-soaked shirt feel cold. A shiver went through him as he walked to the bunkhouse. Joshua was coming from the barn, where he had been husking corn.

"How's it coming with the corn?" he asked.

"We'll have plenty for cornbread and mush this winter. And still enough to keep the horses fat," Joshua said proudly.

Most meals were eaten as a group. Bart's side was the bigger of the two, and had the better stove, so a large table had been set up. Prayers were said before every meal at the request of Sara.

Millie's eyes were smiling as they began eating. "I see you are starting the house early."

The big man nodded as he swallowed a large bite of bread. "I got to thinking, we really don't need to wait until spring to build. Being caught up on the work, now seemed like a good time."

"Yes, Boss Bart," Joshua said. "Even if we only get the walls up, it will cut the wind when heating wash water in the fireplace."

They were all in agreement that starting the new house was a good idea.

CHAPTER NINE

It was into September and the walls were up on the house. Each day, Bart devoted most of his time to shaping each log with the broad-axe and notching it with the double-bit axe. The weather was cooler and hard work felt good.

Nate and Mary had taken over the responsibility of caring for the chickens. One of the hens had hatched a brood of chicks and there was much excitement watching the small, yellow puffs of feathers.

Millie and Sara were busy canning late vegetables. The potatoes and turnips were in the barn's root cellar. Joshua was responsible for caring for the horses and checking on the longhorns. When he finished with that, he helped with the new house.

It was a warm Sunday and they all sat out having a picnic near the brook. The children braved the cold water and splashed in the shallows. Joshua let Bart know about two horses that were missing.

"I just don't know why they would wander

away, Boss Bart," he said.

"Let's enjoy the day. I will go and find them first thing in the morning," Bart said, trying to calm Joshua's concerns. He knew that the man was responsible for taking care of the stock and feared disappointing the boss.

Millie had made a dove pot pie using birds shot by Joshua. Sara made a thick cornbread served with wild berry jam. There was green tomato pie for dessert.

This was the first time Bart had experienced a family gathering like this. He felt an inner warmth, knowing that there would be many more in his future. It was unlikely that he and Millie would ever have children, but he could enjoy watching the playfulness of Nathaniel and Mary.

That night, Bart and Millie lay talking for hours. She kept coming back to thanking him for taking her away from the saloon life. He would change the subject to their building a home together. He knew she had saved him from self-destruction, living the life of a drunk. A friend, Oli, had given him the vision, and she had given him the will.

He could hear Joshua feeding the horses when he woke up. Millie lay sleeping, her hair spilling over the pillow. Quietly, he slipped out of bed. Carrying his boots and clothes to the far side of the room, he dressed quickly. Grabbing his gun belt from its peg, he stepped out into the cool, misty morning. The air smelled of rain.

Sara was fussing with flower beds in front of the bunkhouse. "I have coffee inside, Mister Bart." Before he could answer, she hurried in and returned with a tin mug and a large slice of jam-covered cornbread.

Walking down to the barn, taking bites of the cornbread and washing it down with coffee, he looked around for Joshua. He could see him a distance away from the corral.

"Over here, Boss Bart," he called.

Drinking the last of the coffee and setting the cup on a bench near the barn, he hurried over. The black man was looking at tracks leading away from the ranch.

"It looks like they were led away by a man on a horse," he said, pointing at the trail.

Bart squatted down, inspecting the sign. The horse being ridden left a distinct track. An end piece of one of the shoes was broken off. The fact that the horses hadn't wandered away told Bart he should have gone after them the day before.

He noticed that the tracks between here and the corral had been brushed out. They were easily missed yesterday. Standing and looking in the direction the horses went, he shook his head.

"It won't be a quick job getting them back. I will pack food for a few days." He noticed the guilty look on Joshua's face. "I want you to be in charge of the ranch while I am gone. Keep your gun close."

Millie sat sleepy-eyed at the table while Bart packed what he needed. "I'm sorry I overslept. I should have made you a hardy breakfast before you left. We even have eggs."

Smiling, he looked at her. "Don't worry, my sweet. I will be back before you know it and we can sit down to a whole plate of eggs."

Giving her a quick kiss, he hurried outside. Joshua had the buckskin saddled with the bedroll tied on. Bart nodded and swung onto the animal.

"The most I will hunt for them is three days out. If I don't find the horses, I will head back and we can come up with another plan." Pausing a moment, he continued in a lower voice. "If by chance, I don't come back, promise me you will take care of Millie."

"I will, Boss Bart. I will."

Turning to ride out, he saw Millie standing by the door with a blanket over her shoulders. He waved, and in return she threw a kiss. At a mile-eating trot, he quickly put the ranch buildings behind him.

Tracking the rider with the horses was not difficult. The person probably thought wiping out the tracks next to the corral would be enough. He kept the buckskin at a trot to make up for the time the rustler had gained. With luck, he was not going too far with the animals. He was heading directly south, probably for Austin.

At noon he stopped to give the horse a breather and some water. He rode up on a rise and looked in the direction the tracks were leading. Swinging off the buckskin, he led it to cool off while he ate some jerky. After a half-hour of walking, he tightened the cinch and got back into the saddle.

Not wanting to kill the buckskin by pushing it too hard, he let it walk. There was a stretch of hardpan where he lost the trail. About a mile later, he picked it up again. The man had switched to one of the stolen horses.

Bart kept Buck moving a little faster than was good for the horse. He found where the man had spent the night. He was now less than a half-day behind. Once again the thief was riding his own horse.

It was dark when the big man had to finally stop. He climbed to the top of a rock outcrop and looked for any sign of a fire. After an hour of watching, he finally went back to where his horse was picketed. He made a small fire and cooked a meal of coffee and fried bacon. Sara had sent Mary over with some more cornbread for him to take. This he soaked in the bacon grease. He was exhausted from the ride and looking forward to curling up in his blankets.

While he cleaned the frying pan, Buck started snorting and stomping. The sound wasn't a challenge but rather the sound of a welcome. More like meeting an old friend.

Tossing the pan down, he went to check on the buckskin. It was looking into the dark. Straining his eyes, Bart tried to look for any type of movement. All of a sudden, he saw a large shadow move. He had his revolver halfway out of his holster when the shadowy figure whinnied.

It was one of the horses that had been taken. It wanted to join the man and his horse, but stayed just out of reach. Deciding to ignore the horse until morning, Bart settled in to sleep. He was up at daybreak and was pleased to see the second lost horse had also wandered in. Fashioning two halters out of his rope, he soon had the animals caught and ready to travel.

Anxious to return, he rode steadily, switching his saddle from one horse to another. It was early evening when he arrived at the stand of pine overlooking the ranch buildings. All was quiet. The other horses stood indifferently in the corral. They were waiting for their hay, which Joshua would bring soon.

As he approached the buildings, he smiled. No one had spotted him yet. They wouldn't expect him back so soon. It would be a good surprise. Rounding the bunkhouse, he swung down and called to Joshua to take the horses to the corral.

He received no answer. For a moment, he was irritated by the lack of response. Then fear clutched his stomach. Someone should have answered him.

Stepping quickly, he burst into the door of the bunkhouse. Stopping, he gasped. Lying in the middle of the floor was the half-naked form of Millie. She was covered with cuts and bruises. What was left of her dress and underclothing were ripped and bloody.

Crossing the floor in two large steps, he knelt beside her. She was alive. He didn't know where to touch or hold her without hurting her more. It was impossible to know the extent of the injuries. What he did know was that she had been savagely raped.

Bart began to shake with rage. He had to do something. "Millie, I'm here. I'm sorry I left you."

Her eyes opened. She tried to move. "Too many . . . four men . . . I . . . I tried." Her eyes closed and she lay still, barely breathing.

Gently holding her near him, Bart knew he had to do something. The cuts needed to be cleaned, the deeper ones bandaged. He needed to get her off the floor. The double bed he had built had a broken footboard. The ten-plate stove had been shoved out of place and the stove pipe had pulled loose.

He needed to find Joshua and Sara to help him. He ran to their door and went in. The room was empty. They were gone. He saw nothing had been damaged, so he rushed back and carefully picked Millie up. He brought her next door and laid her in Joshua and Sara's bed. Pulling the covers over her, he then put kindling into the small stove.

As the flames leaped up, he placed a pot of water to heat. He returned to Millie and started to remove her torn clothing. He shuddered when he noticed that two of her finger nails were ripped back and nearly tore off. She had several wounds on her hands and forearms. She had fought whoever attacked her. She had said four were involved.

The water began to boil. Taking clean towels from a shelf, he dipped them in the water and began to clean the wounds. Bart's throat hurt as he fought back the urge to cry. Millie's only reactions were groans when the more severe cuts were cleaned. Someone had used a knife on her, slashing rather than stabbing. There was evidence that she had been struck by some type of club. There were lash marks across her thighs and legs.

With hands shaking almost uncontrollably, he bathed her, removing the blood and evidence of the men who had abused her. The rage he felt at first was replaced with fear for Millie. She was drifting in and out of consciousness. Most of what she said made no sense. He did hear "the slave hunter," and "four men," several times.

Her eyes would open, but did not focus on anything. Bart put one of Sara's night gowns on her. He sat on the edge of the bed and held her close, feeling tremors go through her body. Her face would twist from pain.

"Millie, I have to get you to the doctor in Waco. I don't know what more I can do for you. I am going to get the wagon ready. I won't be gone but a minute." Kissing her softly on the forehead, Bart hurried to the corral to get the team.

It was getting late and the sun was going down.

He would have to risk traveling the road at night. He realized that bouncing along in the wagon might do additional damage.

He tossed hay into the wagon bed to make it softer. He led the team and wagon to the door.

"Bart, Bart, help me, don't . . . don't hurt me. Help me."

The screams came from Millie. Dropping the reins, he ran to her side. She was sitting up in the bed sobbing and swinging her arms. He deflected her arms and he moved to hold her.

"It's me, Bart. I'm here. I will protect you." She struggled for a moment more before sagging against him, trembling. He held her until the shaking stopped. Bart's eyes burned and his throat ached. He continued to speak softly to Millie.

Wrapping the covers from the bed around her, he gently lifted her and brought her to the wagon. It was full dark and the sky was studded with stars. He turned the team onto the road to Waco. He kept them walking to soften the bumps.

Millie began to wail and call his name. Bart stopped the team and climbing onto the back of the wagon.

"Hold me, Bart. Hold me, it's so cold. My head . . . it hurts so."

She was awake. It was too dark to see more than the pale outline of her face. The big man curled up close to her, trying to share his body heat with her.

"They took Joshua and his family. The same foul man as before. You have to help them, Bart. You have to help them," she said in a raspy voice.

"Who did this to you, Millie?" he asked.

"Four men, I fought them, scratched them.

They were too strong . . ." She began to cry softly, "It hurts, my head hurts." Her voice was barely a whisper.

Bart had never been a very religious man. His father would drink and abuse him and his brother on Saturday and then force them to go to church on Sunday. He had watched his friend Oli reach out to the heavens for strength.

Millie began to tremble again. Holding her in his arms, he looked into the night sky. "I am not asking for myself, but for this defenseless woman. She lived the only life she knew how. She loved and gave of herself. If her time has come, please let her be with you. Punish me, not her. I need, . . . we need help. Let me know you are with us."

She squeezed his arm and sighed. And just like that, Millie was gone. He felt the life ebb out of her and peace come to her body.

Was this an answer from heaven? Was she taken to be with God? Bart could not stand the pain in his throat any longer and let the tears flow. His tears ran down his face and the drops splashed on her still, soft, pale cheeks. As he sat there holding his lost love, the moon rose over the horizon, bathing the ranch in a soft glow.

CHAPTER TEN

Bart stood over the grave. Since Millie had died the night before, the fear that he had felt had turned to anger. The smile that had frequented his face over past months was gone. He promised her that he would find the men who did this, making sure that they never had the chance to hurt another woman.

The grave was near a grove of oak trees. Bart vowed that he would bring her a fitting stone, so all who passed would know who lay beneath this dirt. He took some of the flowers Sara had planted in front of the bunkhouse and moved them to her grave. He then marked it with three stones at the head.

Brushing his hands on his pants, Bart said words over her. He knew others could do a better job, but the words he said came from his heart.

Walking from the grave, he took care of the last few things he needed to do before heading for Waco. The chickens were released. He packed the things he would need. He noticed that Joshua's revolver was missing. So were the leg irons that had been left in the lean-to. None of the tracks he saw were familiar.

He went through the tasks almost mechanically. Bart realized that what he'd hoped to have here was over. Most everything, including the cattle, would have to be left. He would drive the horses to Waco and sell them for whatever he could quickly get. He could then hunt every one of the savage animals who'd hurt Millie and kill them.

While readying the horses to be driven to Waco, he noticed that Joshua's mustang and Millie's gray were gone. He guessed that the slave hunter had used them to carry the blacks.

Riding away from the ranch also took its emotional toll. The security of having a home was broken for the second time in his life. He rode into Waco and drove the animals straight to the livery. He left with the buckskin and less money than his horses had been worth. He rode to the saloon and tied Buck to the hitching rail.

Walking up to the bar, he slapped some money on the bar. "Give me a bottle." The pain within him was too much to bear. He needed a drink to ease the ache.

While he drank the first bottle, he told Tony, the bartender, what had happened at the ranch. He ordered a second bottle and the rest of the night became a blur.

* * *

Bart woke and looked around. His head was pounding and his stomach was turning. The way he felt was all too familiar. He smelled of vomit and his face was bruised, one eye almost swollen closed.

He was in a small, windowless room, lying on a narrow bunk. Supplies used in the saloon were stacked against one wall. He sat on the edge of the bed, holding his aching head. He thought, *Maybe a drink might help.*

He stood up, steadying himself against the wall. Pushing the door open, he saw the morning light coming through the fly-specked windows. The bartender was just finishing up his morning chores, readying the saloon for the noon crowd.

Clearing his throat, Bart croaked, "I need a drink."

Tony walked over to the potbelly stove and poured a mug of coffee. Setting it on a table near Bart, he turned and went behind the bar. "What you need is some strong coffee to clear your head."

"What the hell!" Bart snapped.

"Axel Gerber is waiting for you to come outside and shoot it out with him. You killed his boy last night."

Bart felt his hip, his gun was missing. "Where's my damn gun?"

"I have it behind the bar. It is ready and loaded. Drink the coffee." Picking up the holster and revolver, he returned to the table. Setting it down, Tony went and poured himself a cup of coffee. Taking a seat across from Bart, he brought him up to date about what had happened during the lapse of memory.

"Throughout the first bottle of rye, you talked about Millie. You told me about her being attacked by four men. She had always brought something special to the saloon here. I don't know anyone that didn't like or respect her."

"The men in here listening to you were quite

upset and there was talk of helping you find the men and hang them. By the time you got into the second bottle, your anger was getting pretty dangerous and everyone was staying clear of you."

"I was hoping you would pass out. I figured the back room would work fine to let you sleep it off."

"You know, Bart, I would usually have run you out after drinking that much, but I just couldn't do it. I had never seen you like that before. You normally just looked for a fight when drunk. Last night you were looking to kill someone."

"It was late when Dieter came in. He had been drinking up the street and was feeling pretty cocky. You were barely on your feet anymore and looked like an easy target. He stood in the middle of the room and asked you, 'Did you bring your whore with you?'."

"There were over a dozen men that were ready to kick his behind for that kind of talk. Leaning against the bar, you told him you were going to kill him for what he had said. Maybe he didn't know she was dead."

"He pulled his gun and shot the hat right off your head. Still leaning on the bar with one hand, you pulled the Dragoon and emptied it in him. You killed him deader than hell. You were raging about Millie and trying to reload your gun. I guess you planned to shoot him some more".

"Staggering toward him, you tripped over a chair and fell flat. Thank God, you were finally out. Before I could get around the bar to drag you back, a few of his friends put the boots to you. They would have killed you, but the other customers stepped in. It had the makings of a brawl."

"The crowd moved outside and Dieter's

friends, being outnumbered, decided to wait and fight another day. A couple of guys dragged the body out and put it over his horse. They took him back to his father. I put you into the back room."

"Axel was in town first thing this morning, looking to kill you. He is waiting for you in the street. It doesn't matter that the boy shot at you first. He believes in an eye for an eye."

Bart took a drink of the coffee. His liquor torn throat and stomach burned from the coffee. He fought the urge to throw up. "I got no fight with Axel. Tell him to go home and bury his son."

"It ain't that easy, Bart. He needs to spill blood, even if it's his own."

The big man stood on unsteady legs. He was in no shape to face Axel Gerber. In the west a man couldn't back away because he wasn't feeling his best. Bart was confident he could kill the elder Gerber in a gunfight. He wasn't as sure that he wouldn't take lead, that could be fatal. Even if he wasn't killed, the recovery time would give the men he was looking for more time to get away.

Walking up to the bar and leaning heavily against it, Bart looked at the bartender. "Pour me a drink to settle me down. Coffee won't do it."

"No, Bart, I know that one drink will lead to another. If you have a couple drinks now, then after the fight, if you survive, you'll be back for several more. That won't help you find the men you want to hunt for."

Bart's jaw tightened. "Don't be preaching to me, damn you. I know if I need . . . want a drink."

The bartender was also a big man. Heavier set, but easily as strong. He had seen what Millie saw in

Bart. The man in front of him had a good heart but no head for drink.

"Now, why don't you get out in the street? Either fight with Axel or reason with him, but don't sit in here climbing into a bottle to find the courage."

The muscles in Bart's arms flexed. He couldn't believe what he just heard. It sounded like Tony had called him a coward. "Damn you, talking to me like that! You best get yourself a gun."

"Kind of getting your gunfights backed up aren't you? You haven't taken care of the one outside and here you are looking for another one," the man said, facing Bart squarely.

Anger soared through his body. Pushing away from the bar, he stumbled to the center of the room. Looking at the bartender, he said, "I'll deal with you after finishing with Axel."

Straightening himself up, he buckled on his gun and walked to the door. Slicking back his hair with his hands, he pushed the door open and stepped into the street.

"You finally wake up from your stupor, Nevell?" Axel Gerber shouted. Standing down the street in front of the mercantile, the neatly dressed rancher stood waiting.

Bart hadn't decided what he was going do, but he did not want to kill the man. The bartender's words came back to him. "Reason with him." Maybe he could.

"Axel, I am going to walk closer to you. I've something to say before we begin shooting."

"You shot my son. You shot him five times. Nothing you say will change my mind. You are going to die today, or by God, I am willing to die trying to make it so."

"I owe you the right to this fight. I shed the blood of your family." Bart continued to walk slowly toward the rancher. "The trouble is I have a life to avenge also. My woman was raped and beaten by four men. Charles Dabney's freed slaves have been taken to be sold using false papers. The life I had hoped to have, is lost forever. I am not afraid to die, Axel. I will even let you have the first shot, but not today. I have to get justice for the murder of Millie. I have to stop the sale of the free slaves."

"When I have done these things, I will come back here and give you your opportunity to settle with me. If I lose the trail of the killers and any chance of finding them, I will return to face you."

"What I am asking you is the time needed to do what I have to, so I can go to my grave, knowing those who killed Millie are punished. As you say, an eye for an eye."

By this time, Bart was only a few feet away from Axel Gerber. If they drew now, they would both die. Probably slowly from being gut-shot. The look of pain on the man's face was the same as Bart felt in his heart. It was an ache that would last the rest of their lives.

Axel swallowed and seemed to wilt a little. Bart repeated his request. "I won't cheat you out of facing your son's killer. I am just asking you for a little time for me to do the same for my Millie."

"Only because I liked Millie, I will wait for you to find her killers. If you don't come back, I will hunt you down."

"Mr. Gerber, I promise you, I will come back or I will be dead."

Near the livery were two of Axel's ranch hands waiting for the outcome of the fight. The elder Gerber stepped away from Bart and waved for the men to bring his horse over.

Accepting the reins of his horse, Axel climbed up into the saddle. He looked over at Bart. "Only because of Millie will I wait. She deserves to have her killers punished." With that, he turned his horse and led his men out of town.

Left standing in the street, Bart felt weak. He settled his hand on the Colt Dragoon. He swallowed hard. The loop was still on the hammer. There was no way that Axel could have missed that. He could have easily won the fight. He must truly want Millie's killers found.

CHAPTER ELEVEN

It felt like a long walk from the mercantile to the saloon. Bart realized that he had followed the sound advice of the bartender after threatening him. Secondly, had he taken a drink, one would have not been enough and there was no doubt that either he or Axel would be dead now.

Stepping into the saloon, he felt a little sheepish. While the words he said to Axel came easy, he didn't have any idea of what to say to Tony. The room was empty. Bart walked to the stove and poured himself coffee. Sitting back at the table, he took a sip. It tasted better.

"There's a bucket of hot water in the back. Go wash yourself. You stink."

Startled by the gruff voice of the bartender, Bart almost choked on his coffee. Coughing, he turned to face Tony. "You were right . . ."

"We ain't got time for jawin'," Tony said, cutting Bart off. "Get cleaned up and I'll get us some grub. Use the clean clothes I put out. You got some fast traveling to do."

Bart realized that he would have to go back to the ranch and try to find the men's trail. That was going to give them another day. Other than looking at some of the tracks left behind, he had only thought about finding a drink after burying Millie.

Wearing the clean shirt and wool trousers, he hurried back into the saloon. He was greeted by the smell of bacon and pancakes. "Just wrap some bacon in a couple of cakes. I have to get back to the ranch and pick up the trail."

"Sit down and eat. I can save you the trip. The men you are looking for came through here after leaving your ranch. What they were talking about didn't make sense until you told me about Millie."

Taking a seat, Bart welcomed the steaming stack of pancakes. "You talk, I'll eat."

"Well, it looks to me like you have two tasks facing you," Tony started. "Two men had been hanging around town. A skinny, sandy-haired fellow named Jonny Tucker, sort of fancied himself a ladies' man. He hung around with a short, wiry, buckskin-clad trapper named Bruno Pascal. Pascal lost an eye fighting the Blackfoot and wears a patch. None of the gals wanted to be with him. They said he treated them bad. Liked to pull his knife and taunt them with it."

"Jonny Tucker was looking for Millie. I guess he had known her from an earlier trip. He was pretty upset when he learned she'd taken up with a rancher. A few days later they were drinking hard with a slave hunter. I overheard the slaver saying he knew where Millie was. He also said you would be gone a couple days. It was a busy night and I had lost track of them. Later, they was playing cards with Dieter and some of the other Gerber hands."

"They played poker until late. I was sure there would be a fight. The boys at Gerber's play a less than honest game. I figured the trapper to be a savvy card player who would pick up on cheats. I was only too glad when the game broke up and they left without busting the place up."

"I was just closing up for the night when I notice Tucker and Pascal in a meet with the slave hunter and some of the Gerber men out on the edge of town. They were still there when I got ready to turn in."

"They had been gone a couple days. I figured they'd moved on. The two came in drunk a couple nights ago. Pascal was scratched up some. I figured some lady finally got in some licks on the mean bastard. Jonny was mighty quiet. A couple of ladies tried to spend some time with him, and he didn't want nothing to do with them."

"They were making plans on heading west. Talked of leaving the next morning. Jonny wanted to head for Santa Fe. Pascal planned to ride with him and continue on to Colorado. I guess he has a wintering place in the mountains."

"I asked Jonny what happened to the slave hunter. He said the man had a load and was heading for Galveston. At the time, I was glad the whole bunch was leaving town. Didn't much care for any of them."

Bart had sat listening to what the bartender was saying, his breakfast forgotten. "That would make three of the four men. By what you say, it sure sounds like they were involved."

"You said that you looked at the tracks. I know the trapper traded his horse at the livery before leaving. You can find out if it was at the ranch," Tony suggested.

"Thanks for the meal, Tony," Bart said. He headed for the door. Stopping abruptly, he turned to the bartender. "Damn, I forgot all about the buckskin. What happened to my horse?"

"You were in no shape to go anywhere, so I brought it to the livery. I had them give it a good rubdown and some extra grain."

"That was good of you. Thank you," Bart said.

"Don't thank me too fast. I told Junior that you would be good for it," the bartender laughed. "Oh, and as far as your gear, it is at the livery also. I will just burn the clothes you changed out of."

Nodding, Bart turned and hurried out the door. It felt good to be back out in the street. His mind was working fast. First, he needed to find Joshua's family and get them back to the ranch. Then he would head for Santa Fe, and if necessary, to the ends of the earth, until the men who hurt Millie were dead.

Junior was going over the horses Bart had brought in from the ranch. He looked up at the big man as he approached. "Good stock you brung in. You know, I didn't know about Millie. She was a favorite at the saloon."

"So I've heard," Bart replied flatly.

"I hope you don't hold the price I paid you against me. Times have been slow."

"I accepted what you offered. I want to see the horse you got from the trapper."

Junior hurried into the livery. "I can give you a real good price on that animal. It's lame right now. Stone bruise on the right front. Should be good as ever in a week or ten days."

Bart stayed near the corral and waited for the hostler to return with the horse. Remaining silent, he watched as the man paraded it back and forth. The animal was in poor shape, having received rough care from the trapper.

Bart recognized the horse's tracks as one that had been at the ranch. He felt the heat of anger. Satisfied, he said, "I'm not looking to buy the animal. I just needed to see the tracks."

"You telling me that Bruno Pascal was part of the trouble at your ranch?" the hostler asked.

"That he was, Junior."

"Explains his hurry to make a deal and get out of town. Believe he left with a man named Jonny Tucker. That Jonny was a good boy in bad company," Junior said, shaking his head.

Bart followed Junior Jones back into the livery and found the buckskin. Its coat shined from the thorough grooming. The gear lay next to the horse's stall. Sliding the Hawken rifle from the scabbard, he checked that it was still loaded. It would have to be cleaned and reloaded to prevent the possibility of a misfire.

With the buckskin saddled and his gear stowed, Bart led the horse to the water trough. While it drank, he went back to find Junior. The man was busy cleaning the stalls with his burro pulling the cart.

"What do I owe you?" he asked.

"Well," Junior said, scratching his head. "Hell, I done okay on the horses. We're all even."

Swinging up into the saddle, Bart looked down at the man. "Next time I need a horse, I'll let you get more even."

Turning the horse south, he trotted out of Waco. He stopped by Wolfgang's to pick up a few supplies, including some extra powder. The man with Joshua's family had also stopped to resupply. He had them riding double on the mustang and gray. Bart found out that the man's name was Smoke. Few people liked him and that included Wolfgang.

Bart handed Wolfgang some extra coins for the supplies. "I need to have a marker made for Millie. This should cover what the stone cutter will charge."

"I'd be glad to do it. A fellow I know does nice work and won't charge too much."

Using a page from a tally book, he wrote what he wanted on the stone, and handed it to Wolfgang. "If I don't come back, go to the ranch and put it on her grave. It's near the oak trees. I marked the head with some stones."

Wolfgang took the paper. Glancing at it, he looked up with surprise.

Leaving the trading post, Bart now had a name along with a face to hate. It was less than a 10 day ride from Galveston. He should be able to travel faster than the slaver. The memory of the lash mark on Millie's legs brought the heat of anger back.

Kicking his heels into the buckskin, he galloped for a while. Slowing the animal back to a walk, he muttered, "Sorry to take it out on you, Buck. When we catch up with that bastard, the measure of pain I will put on him will be great."

The Brazos River would take him most of the way. Then he would cut over to the Buffalo Bayou until Harrisburg, just east of the new city named after Sam Houston. From there he would continue to Galveston Bay. That's where Smoke planned to sell the slaves. Most likely he had forged ownership papers.

Bart hoped that he could catch them before traveling all the way to Galveston. With the tracks being several days old and a fair amount of travelers using the same trails, finding any sign would be unlikely.

As he passed each campsite, Bart spent a few moments looking them over. He hoped to find something that would point to Joshua or his family. By the end of the first day, he had traveled over 40 miles. It was dark when he made camp. The well-groomed coat of the buckskin was now dust and sweat-covered.

The moon was just coming up when he had the horse rubbed down and on the picket rope. He sat under a spreading oak tree, with a small fire. His coffee pot was sitting on a flat stone next to the fire. He chewed on a piece of jerky while swatting mosquitoes and waiting for the water to come to a boil.

While today's search was not fruitful, he was pleased with the distance they had traveled. The horse was still in top shape and should be able to go several long days before the strain of the trip began to wear it down.

Finishing his meal with coffee and bread he had gotten from Wolfgang, Bart leaned against the oak and listened to the night noises. A lonesome bullfrog called into the night, hoping to attract a mate. An owl hooted in a tree just downstream.

After bringing the buckskin closer to camp, he spread his bedroll and curled up under the covers. Glancing at the sky, he saw that the clouds were moving in, hiding the stars.

Bart woke to heavy dew and fog. He had slept longer than he had wanted to. Quickly, he rolled up his bed roll. His plans for making a hot breakfast were gone. He drank the cold, stale coffee and finished the bread.

With the buckskin saddled, he looked out into

the fog. He would have to travel a bit slower until it lifted. He couldn't afford a misstep by his horse. The sound of the horse's hooves seemed unusually loud in the fog enclosed world as they rode. The only other thing he could hear was the bell on a boat on the Brazos River, hoping to warn other watercraft of their position.

Finally, Bart was forced to dismount and lead the horse. The fog was so thick that he was unable to see the ground from atop the buckskin. The air was heavy with moisture. It felt like if he opened his mouth it would fill with water.

It was mid-morning when a breeze came up and the fog lifted. The sky remained hazy with low-hanging clouds. It was still early, so Bart kept Buck at a trot. Lightning was flashing in the western sky. A fast-moving storm was headed his way.

"Damn the luck, Buck," he said. "It's not like we have much of a chance of picking up a trail, but with the rain, it will make it almost impossible."

By noon he had donned his slicker and was being buffeted by waves of windblown rain. The temperature had dropped, yet Bart felt clammy inside the slicker. The horse walked steadily, its head bobbing up and down with each step.

He would have to stop soon and rest the horse. With the heavy rain, he wouldn't be able to make a meal. Swinging down under a grove of pecan trees, he loosened the horse's cinch and dug for some jerky in the saddlebags. The western sky was still thick with rain-laden, dark clouds. Lightning was flashing all around him, resulting in powerful booms of thunder.

The buckskin tended to react to the closer rumbles. Bart knew that he couldn't stay under the trees. It would be a quick end to his search if lightning struck the tree above him. Lowering the brim of his hat, he led the horse away from the shelter of the grove.

For over an hour he walked, his boots slipping on the muddy trail. Finally, the storm blew by him. He was drenched under the rain slicker. The sun came out in the afternoon sky, quickly turning the rain-soaked countryside into a humid oven.

He removed his wool shirt and wrung it out. Tying it to his bedroll, he planned to hang it to dry overnight. Rubbing the water off the steaming horse with his broad hands, he then tightened the cinch. Climbing into the saddle, he headed back down the trail.

For two long days, with short nights of rest, the man and horse continued toward Galveston. He came to the community of Peck. There was a saloon that had rooms for travelers. It was still a couple of hours until dark, but he decided that both he and the horse could use some rest.

The area had rolling hills and several stands of pine trees. He saw fields with beans ready for harvest. He rode up to the saloon and tied the horse to a porch post. Entering the building, he saw several farmers and businessmen enjoying a drink or two before heading for home. Many were speaking German, a language Bart did not recognize.

Standing at the end of the bar, he waited for the bartender to work his way down to him. Setting a glass and bottle in front of Bart, he said, "The rye is good, but we have a beer as good as *Spaten* back in Germany."

Holding his hand up to indicate that he didn't want a drink, Bart said, "I need a meal, a room, and a place to put my horse. Can you help me?"

"Ja, it is eight bits. If you want grain for the horse, that would be another two bits. My wife has lamb in the oven. Be ready soon."

Quickly, the transaction was taken care of and Bart led the buckskin to the stable behind the saloon. He noticed an outhouse near the stable and took a moment to use it before tending to the horse. He was pleased to see the stack of older newspapers for reading or taking care of business after going. It beat squatting in the bush.

With the horse rubbed down and enjoying a generous serving of grain, Bart headed for the bucket of water and washbasin next to the back door of the saloon. Taking time to wash the sweat from his head and neck, he then used the clean, thread-bare towel to dry.

He carried his saddlebags and rifle to the room. It was small, but very clean and had the smell of lye. The curtains were ironed, and the bed was covered with a colorful quilt. He was concerned about sitting on the edge of the bed with his dusty clothes.

Leaving his gear safely stowed next to the bed, he returned to the saloon and sat at a table that allowed a good view of the room. The temptation to have the saloon keeper bring over a bottle was almost overwhelming.

A plump and pretty sandy-blond girl came to the table. "Günther says you paid for your supper. Helen will have the food ready in a minute. How about a stein of beer while you wait?"

Feeling mighty parched after the day's ride, he decided one would not hurt. "I'll have one only. And then if you would bring me some coffee." As the pert girl turned to go, he repeated, "Just one drink, no more."

The brew was light and refreshing. The barrels were stored in a cellar below the bar, which kept the beer nicely cool. He would have liked more, but he knew that one would lead to another and the night, maybe several days, would be lost before he sobered up.

The bartender's wife, Helen, was a mighty good cook. The lamb was juicy and tender. It was served with some type of squash and a generous portion of greens. As asked for, a pot of coffee came with the meal.

With the crowd waning, Günther left the bartending to a hired man. He sat with Bart and poured himself a mug of coffee. "After a long night slinging rye and beer, it feels good to sit and enjoy some coffee."

"Your wife is a good cook," Bart said, complimenting the meal.

"We come over from Germany in 1835. Been married 30 years. Started this place in '40. She does love to cook. Helen really gets a lot of pleasure watching people eat her food."

The man's words caused a pang of regret in Bart. He would never be able to reflect back on him and Millie being together for years.

"I'm looking for a man named Smoke. Big man, rides a paint, carries a whip and hunts runaways."

"Was he toting a family of slaves?" Günther asked.

"Would have been a man and woman with two younguns," Bart replied.

"Saw the man a day ago. He bought a bottle

and some food he took with him. The black man was pretty well beat up. They was all pretty scared. Heard him threaten to hang the man if he tried anything again."

Bart sat, his teeth clenched. The sighting of those he searched for was a relief, but hearing about the condition of Joshua was maddening.

He had witnessed cruelty to slaves at the hands of his own father. Knowing that the four of them were in the animal's hands sent rage and fear coursing through him.

"Does anyone know what road they took leaving town?" he asked.

"Only one choice if you're heading to Galveston. You pick it up near the Buffalo Bayou. It runs alongside of Harrisburg. 'Course now they call it Houston, after the general."

Drinking the last of his coffee, Bart set the cup down and pushed back from the table. "I best get to sleep. I want to be on the road by daylight."

The perky sandy-blond walked by him, carrying six mugs of beer. She smiled and said, "Sure you don't want another before calling it a night?"

Trying to smile, he shook his head. "No, not tonight."

Günther leaned back on his chair. "I will have Helen make you something to eat before you leave. I haven't asked you why you are looking for this man named Smoke, but by the look on your face when I mentioned the man was beaten, I can imagine it is personal."

"They were free slaves and friends of mine." Bart replied.

"When you get this Smoke, stop back with

your friends. I will let them stay in the room with you."

With that, Günther got up and went behind the bar. His offer did not go unnoticed by Bart. Blacks were not allowed to sleep in the hotels. They most often spent the night with the owner's horses in the stable.

He walked into the tidy room and kicked off his boots. Removing his pants and shirt, he looked at the bright white sheets on the bed. "I'm still too damn dirty to sleep in this bed," he muttered.

The bed was too short for the big man. The foot board had an opening that was wide enough to stick his feet through. Lying on the soft mattress, covered with the clean sheets and down-filled comforter, Bart lay awake, unable to fall asleep.

He didn't know if it was the coffee or knowing he was getting close to the slave hunter. Regardless, he tossed and turned in the most comfortable bed he had ever slept in. His mind raced as he thought about what might still happen to Joshua and his family. He hoped death didn't come too fast to Smoke.

CHAPTER TWELVE

Helen was awake and had boiled eggs and fried ham waiting for him when he got up. It was served with thick slices of bread covered with strawberry preserves. Wolfing the meal down and chasing it with coffee, he thanked her and headed for the stable.

He found the buckskin saddled and ready for travel. Günther smiled and nodded when he saw Bart. "Wanted to save you some time."

Bart was filled with mixed emotions. The kindness shown by Günther and Helen had been a complete surprise. His thoughts moved back and forth between Smoke and the saloon owners. He felt fury and then warmth.

After he rode away, he shouted, "Damn it, I want to stay mad. I need to stay mad!"

The buckskin snorted, startled by the outburst.

When the sun came up, Bart was miles away from Günther's saloon. The road was in better shape than the ones he had ridden on before. Many of them had been little more than trails. The buckskin was willing to keep on going. It had lost weight on the trip. Having too little time to graze and rest was taking its toll.

Almost unexpectedly, he found the first solid

proof that he was close. He pulled the buckskin off the road to take a breather. He also needed to relieve himself. Stopping near an old cottonwood, he looped the reins around some scrub brush.

Standing there enjoying the moment, he noticed a place just beyond the tree where some horses had been tied. Finishing quickly, he buttoned his fly as he walked toward the spot. The horse's tracks were plain and he recognized the prints of the mustang and gray. The third set would be the paint.

Feeling the excitement surge through him, he looked the area over. They had camped there the night before. He found where the blacks had been chained, forced to relieve themselves where they slept.

An empty can of beans lay near a dead fire. There was little evidence that Joshua's family had been fed any amount. He continued to move around the camp. There was a pine tree away from the fire that had the bark ripped from it. Smoke had stripped it with his whip, no doubt to terrorize his captives.

Knowing that he was getting close made Bart anxious to move on. He forced himself to continue looking for anything that might help on the search. He was now a day's ride from Galveston. The town and bay area was large and could make finding Joshua's location near impossible.

Finally, behind the tree the family had been chained to, he spotted lettering. Scratched in the dirt was the word 'FISHA', and next to it, 'ASTINA'. It had to be from Joshua. He had hoped Bart would follow. This had to be their destination near Galveston.

Riding away from the cottonwood, he felt anticipation, knowing the hunt was almost over. He realized that finding the camp was luck. To find the men who had beaten Millie, he would need a large helping of luck. Being driven by anger could help him continue on, but without a few breaks he would be like a blind man running in a forest.

A half-day away from Galveston, he was riding in full dark. Off to the right he saw a lit window. Turning Buck in that direction, he made out a log cabin and the outline of a barn just beyond.

Stopping the horse just short of the place, he called out, "Hello, the cabin. Can I come in?"

The lamp was snuffed out and a moment later he heard the door creak open slightly. "Who's out there?" a gruff voice said.

"My name is Bart Nevell. I hail from Waco and am headed for Galveston. I need a place to spend the night," he answered.

The door creaked again as it was opened a little more. "Git off the hoss and walk careful like to me. Keep your hands away from your sides."

Moving slowly, Bart dismounted and move toward the cabin. The moon moved out from behind a cloud and finally he could see the bearded, stoop shouldered man. He held a rifle or shotgun, but it was not pointed at him.

"I have been on the road for over a week and could use a place to sleep, and a meal."

"I already et, but got a little something still near the hearth. I'll light a lamp so's we can take your hoss inta the barn."

Lighting a stick from his cook stove, he lit the lamp and showed Bart the way, careful to stay slightly behind the big man. The old man hung the lamp on a peg and stepped back while Bart removed the saddle and rubbed down the buckskin.

"Ya take good care of your hoss. It's a sign of a good man."

"Thanks," Bart said. "I got lots of miles ahead of me and want to keep the horse fit."

"Over in the barrel is some grain. Give the hoss some," the man offered.

Finishing up with the animal, Bart slung his saddlebags over his shoulder and carried the Hawken in his left hand. "I gave you my name. What do I call you?"

"Wilbert Henny is the name, just call me Wil," the old man said.

Walking across the dusty yard, Wil spit out a spent chew of tobacco and then tore a fresh chunk from a braided plug pulled from his pocket.

"Do you chaw?" he asked, extending the plug to Bart.

"No thanks. I could do with some of that chow you mentioned."

The cabin was small and in need of a good cleaning. A knife-scarred table with two chairs sat next to the fireplace. A rumpled cot was across the room in the corner. A couple pegs were pounded into the wall and held Wil's extra clothes. Two small barrels with a rough plank across them served as a place to store pots and supplies.

Wil moved the blackened pot of stew closer to the coals. A coffee pot already sat next to the heat. "It should only take a minute to warm it back up."

He stood over the pot and stirred the contents, his tobacco-stained beard just inches away from the top. Dipping a wooden spoon into the thick stew, the old man took a taste.

"Yes sir, I do make a mighty fine rabbit stew," he boasted.

Bart nodded and smiled, hoping that the tobacco juice wasn't one of the things that made it taste good.

The coffee was already hot and Wil poured two cups and set them on the table. Sitting and drinking the coffee, they waited for the stew to heat. Bart heard the story about the old man coming to the area and building the place. He heard about hard times and crop failures.

Finally, Wil got up and scooped the stew into a clay bowl. He set the warmed stew in front of Bart. He then went and got a couple of sourdough rolls and set them next to the stew.

"Eat up. I was saving the biscuits for morning, but the stew is best with them." Seeing Bart's hesitation to start, he waved his arms. "Eat up before it gets cold."

The old man was right, the stew was good. He also missed having someone to talk to. Wil kept up a constant stream of chatter throughout the meal. At the end of each story, he would spit into the pail next to him.

With his meal finished, Bart stared at the grizzled old man. His greasy, food-stained shirt hung loosely out of his baggy pants. His boots were down at the heel, and one had a split in the toe, probably caused by an axe.

Wil was just finishing the story about bagging a cat that was attacking young stock. Before he had the chance to launch into another tale, Bart broke in. "I am looking for a man named Smoke, who is bringing some slaves to market."

"Don't know nobody named Smoke," the man said, spitting into the pail.

"He may be headed for Astina, to a place called Fisha."

"Yep, that would be Austinia where he'd go with slaves. They got cages to keep them in until you go to market. Lots of slavers use Fisher's. You know, one time . . ."

Bart cut him off, being impatient for more information. "When would he take them to market?"

"Well, let's see, today's Wednesday. Auctions are held Friday and Saturday." With hardly a pause, Wil continued the story he had been interrupted on.

After another hour of stories, Bart found it difficult to keep his eyes open. He got up and spread his blanket roll in front of the fireplace.

"I got an early start tomorrow. Best I get some sleep." He then kicked off his boots and wrapped himself in his blankets.

Wil turned down the lamp and went out for a bit. When he returned, he looked at Bart and said, "Checked on the stock after using the little house. They are all set."

Bart pretended to be asleep, and listened to the old man grunt and wheeze as he got ready for bed.

The rising sun found Bart saddling the buckskin. Wil poked his head out of the cabin door. "Got coffee ready. Porridge will be done in a minute."

Though he was anxious to get going, Bart knew he should eat. As he feared, the meal took over an hour. Some of the old stories were told by Wil, and some new. The old man followed him all the way to the barn, telling one last story.

As Bart turned the buckskin toward the trail,

Wil called out, "Stop by on yer way back."

Bart waved and smiled. Inside, he promised himself that he would ride wide of the cabin.

As described by Wil, the Fisher place was north and west of Galveston. It was no more than five miles from the cabin. After riding out of sight of the cabin, he stopped and checked his Colt Dragoon and Hawken. He then pulled the knife from his boot and ran his thumb across the blade. It was razor sharp.

As ready as he could hope to be, he rode to find the Fisher place. He had to skirt areas of salt marshes and cross several creeks that emptied into Galveston Bay. The dirt road was well-maintained, with logs or planks laid across wet areas.

Bart began to pass farm fields of beans or squash. Dozens of slaves worked picking and hauling produce to waiting wagons. There were impressive farm houses with split-rail fences extending from them to pasture horses.

On a rise west of Galveston Bay, he could see ships lying at anchor. There were two longboats loaded with chained slaves being rowed to one of the ships. They would probably end up on plantations in Georgia or the Carolinas.

He waved down a buggy being pulled by a large, shiny black horse. The driver was a white-haired man with a trimmed moustache. He carried a small bag that probably had medical supplies.

"Excuse me," Bart said, "can you tell me where I can find the Fisher place?"

Nodding, the old man answered, "Sure can. I just came from there, checked over some new blacks before the auction."

"Was there one named Joshua?" Bart asked.

"Don't get into monikers. Just stay on this road about two miles. You'll see a green clapboard building. That's the Fisher. The smell will reach you before you reach it."

Thanking the man, Bart urged his horse into a trot. He had no idea of what he was going to do when he came face to face with Smoke. He hadn't found the papers proving Joshua'a family were free. It wouldn't matter. Bart had no intention of leaving the area without the family.

True to the old man's word, the putrid smell was heavy in the air before the building came into sight. The green paint was peeling. A wide porch ran the length of the front of the dwelling. Several iron strap cages sat in the back of the building. Most had multiple occupants. Beyond the cages was a rubbish pile. The decaying body of a slave lay near it, waiting for disposal.

Bart swung down at the hitching rail in front of the building. He could hear crying, wailing, and even singing coming from behind the house. Two rough-looking characters carrying scatter guns lounged on the porch. One of them stepped toward the big man.

"What can we do ya for?"

Taking a chance, Bart said, "I'm supposed to meet Smoke this afternoon. I'm running a little early."

Turning to fuss with the cinch on the buckskin, he could hear one man walking up behind him.

"Smoke went down to the wharf for some tequila and women. He ain't s'pose to be back until Friday."

Turning to face the man, Bart casually replied, "Probably that was where I was to meet him. I just need to check on the blacks and then I'll go find him."

"No one but them that brings them in goes to the pens," the scurvy-looking man said. Bart noticed his confederate moving closer.

Towering a full head above the man, he stared coldly. "Smoke and I both got money in them blacks. I stayed behind to clean up a mess while he went ahead. He tends to be rough on the stock. I need to make sure they are fit for the auction coming up."

Being born with a natural scowl and the years of sun and wind taking any signs of softness from his face, Bart stood over the man, waiting for an answer.

The man stepped back, deciding he'd rather bend a rule than face the wrath of the big man in front of him. "Make it quick. When you get to the Harpoon, tell Smoke to let us know of any partners next time."

Waving the other man back, he turned and went back onto the porch. As the man left, Bart noticed a window curtain move back and the face of a pale, dark-haired woman appeared. The big man touched his hat and nodded at her. Quickly, the curtain closed.

"Damn strange place this is," he muttered.

As he approached the cages, the smell all but turned his stomach. There were no toilet facilities. The dirt was wet and slick with the blacks' waste. Most of the occupants did their best to keep the filth out of the cages. Each had a water bucket and empty bowls in one corner. Bart passed one cage that had an ill man lying in his own excrement, unable to help himself.

Most were in acceptable shape. Very few of the men had shirts. The women wore simple sack dresses. Lash marks at various levels of healing were on many of the naked backs. In all, there were about 20 cages. Each could hold up to six slaves. They all wore the blank stare of helplessness.

Joshua saw Bart first. "Boss, massa Bart. Over here."

The big man was not prepared for what he saw. The family was sitting on the straw-littered floor of the cage. Joshua was cut and bloody. Several lash marks covered all sides of his body. Sara sat, head hanging, her dress torn and blood-splattered. One eye was swollen half-shut. The children had less physical damage, but they sat cowering on the far side of the cage.

Knowing he was being watched from the house, Bart knew enough to act the part of an owner. Memories from his youth along with what Smoke had done to this family, made it almost impossible to speak coherently.

"What in God's name has that fool done to my property?" he shouted. "Smoke has damn near ruined the auction value of these blacks."

Raising his voice was helping him from boiling over and doing something stupid. "Has the damn doctor looked them over?"

Turning to the house, he bellowed, "Someone bring something to clean 'em up. For Christ sake, I need to get them fixed or they'll be in worse shape than the sickly one lying in the bottom of the other cage."

Suddenly, the back door opened and the woman whose face he had seen in the window hurried toward him, covering her nose with a perfumed hanky. She carried a bucket of water and a bundle with liniment, brown soap, and some rags.

She set them down in front of him and hissed, "This is how your friend brought them in. There will be an extra charge."

"That's no damn excuse," Bart snapped. "I also want extra straw and food brought to them. I'll deal with Smoke on their condition. When I come back on Friday, they best be looking ready to sell."

For a moment, the two were locked in an angry stare, Bart's face red with veins bulging, the woman's face sharp and even whiter if possible. Finally, she made a snorting noise and hurried back to the building.

His muscles quivering from the confrontation, Bart found that he was more in control of his anger. The shouting had helped relieve the pressure. He moved the bundle and bucket next to the cage.

In a low voice, he said, "Clean yourselves up. I'll take care of Smoke and will be back to take you home."

He then strode back to the buckskin. Finding one of the rough-looking men checking out his gear, he grabbed the man by the back of his jacket and shoved him over the hitching rail, sending him sprawling into the dirt.

The other man started to bring up the scatter gun. Bart pulled his revolver, pointing it at the man. "You bring that son-of-a-bitch up and I will send you to hell."

The man froze a moment and then lowered the gun. Swinging into the saddle, Bart turned the buckskin to leave. Out of the corner of his eye, he saw the curtain move. The shrew was still watching.

CHAPTER THIRTEEN

The wharf consisted of several rough-looking saloons and taverns, a few brightly painted brothels, and some seedy boarding houses or hotels. The lice-infested beds were used to bring girls or sleep off a drunk. The Harpoon was located near the center of all the mayhem.

It was barely past noon when Bart stopped across the street from the establishment. Up and down the street were men lying or sitting, unable to move under their own power. Some were victims of bad booze, others from opium brought in by sailors.

He had stopped in front of a weather-scarred mercantile. Tying the buckskin to the rail, Bart went inside. He picked up a few supplies, including canned peaches, a shirt, a simple dress, and some peppermint sticks.

"You'll get a woman faster with rye than with store-bought candy," the shopkeeper snickered.

"Jest tally up the supplies and keep your gab to yourself," he answered coldly.

Taken aback by the response, the man hurried and filled the order. It was put into an empty flour bag. "That will be $6.00. Care for anything else?"

Avoiding more conversation, he tossed the

coins onto the counter. Bart picked up the bundle and stepped out into the street. The air was hot and humid. It would be hours before the sea breezes would pick up.

Tying the bundle to the back of the saddle, he grabbed the reins. Leading the buckskin, he walked along the street looking for a livery. A lady looking for an early customer was disappointed when he declined her offer, but she did point the way to a livery.

A balding man with a scar extending from below his right eye to the tip of his chin came when Bart called out. He flashed a toothless, crooked smile upon seeing a potential customer.

"Cully at your service. Pardon the face. I didn't duck in time when a horse kicked. Doc said I was lucky it didn't take my nose off. Would have been a shame to lose my smeller."

"Need my horse put up for a day or two. May have to leave in a hurry," Bart said.

"It'll be a buck for two days, in advance. We got mold-free hay and corn," the hostler boasted.

With the deal set, Buck followed the man. The barn was more stifling than outside. Leading the buckskin to a stall, Bart stripped the saddle and began brushing the horse. While doing so, he looked around to see if Smoke had his horses here. They were not in the livery.

"I saw a nice-looking paint around town a couple days ago," Bart said, fishing for information.

"That would be Heller's horse. It's in the corral out back with a couple others he had. Nasty bastard that one is. Doesn't take very good care of his horses."

Bart didn't know Smoke's last name. Heller

might not be his real name either. He might have needed it to get papers on the slaves. "You think he would be willing to sell it?"

"Good chance he'd sell the other two. He brung some blacks in with the gray and mustang. Once sold, he won't need 'em. Where are you staying? I will send him over if I see him," Cully said.

"Haven't got a place yet. Thought I might sleep in your hayloft."

"That will cost you two bits, in advance," the man said, flashing his toothless smile.

Bart had passed a place called Ma's Kitchen on his way to the livery. Settling up with Cully, he went to hunt up a meal.

Ma was a fat, sloppy, wiry-haired man. He was shirtless and had an apron tied around his neck. He was sitting at one of the tables, cutting vegetables to add to a soup. Bart watched as far too much of the peels and stems found their way into the pot.

Taking a seat at a table that gave him a good view of the Harpoon's front door, he waited for the man to look up.

"I need something to eat. Hopefully not the soup you are working on," Bart said.

"Got some fish, fresh from the boats. Could fry you a mess up with a couple eggs," he said, wiping his face and forehead with the bottom of his apron.

"Make it four eggs," the big man replied.

Sitting and watching the dusty street baking in the afternoon sun, he could hear the man rattling the stove and pans. The smell of cooking made Bart's stomach growl. It had been many hours since he'd eaten at the cabin.

The cook came out with a large tin plate. There

were three pan fish next to four grease-covered eggs. Setting it down in front of Bart, he went back in the kitchen and returned with a mug of coffee.

"That'll be two bits."

"In advance, I suppose," Bart said sarcastically.

The man stood with his hand out, sweat running down his face. Handing the man a coin, Bart started in on the food.

The fish were poorly scaled and boney. When his father had taken him fishing, the elder Nevell had called this type of catch, butter fish. Bart had always assumed it was because they were floured and fried in butter. He decided that the fish in front of him had little flour and had not seen butter.

Taking his time to pick as much of the flesh as possible from the boney meal, he continued to watch the street. The eggs were runny and most of their goodness drained out of the three prong fork he was using.

"You got any biscuits or bread back there?" Bart asked.

Grunting, the man got up and retrieved two biscuits from the kitchen. Setting them down, he hesitated, debating if he could charge for them. Looking at the cold eyes of Bart, he decided to include them in the meal.

Bart looked the biscuits over. Both had some green growth. Pinching off the mold, he soaked up the eggs with the stale, crumbling bread.

With the meal finished, he requested another cup of coffee. Not that it tasted good, but it was to kill time to watch the Harpoon. The cook moved his operation to the kitchen. Bart doubted that he would see him again.

As the afternoon waned, the wharf began to come alive. Business owners swept the mud from the walks and some tossed buckets of mop water out into the street. A few working girls appeared, lounging near the drinking establishment.

Unable to sit on the uncomfortable chair any longer, Bart walked out into the street. He went toward the Harpoon. Hesitating a moment at the open door, he decided to go in and look the room over.

The dim room smelled of spilt beer and cigar smoke. A poor attempt had been made at sweeping the plank floor. Marred tables and chairs sat waiting for hard-drinking, card-playing patrons. A long bar ran across the back of the room. An impressive mirror with the image of a harpoon was mounted behind the bar.

The bartender was finishing up tapping a keg of beer for the night's business. "I'll test that brew for you," Bart called out.

Drawing a foamy cup of the amber liquid, he set it on the bar for Bart. "First draw is free," he said, smiling. Turning away, he went to stock bottles of rye on the back bar.

Sipping the beer, Bart turned to face the room. Soon it would be a bedlam of sailors and longshoremen, letting off steam after a hard day's work. Four girls who worked the customers came in, chatting and laughing. They continued through the saloon and went into a back room.

The thud of boots on the walk and the loud voices of a group of men came toward the Harpoon. Not wanting to be noticed, Bart moved into a darkened corner and took a seat. Lowering his hat brim a bit, he continued sipping his beer.

The rough and tumble men came through the door, shouting to the bartender for drinks. One called to the girls in the back to come out and have a drink. The scene was repeated over and over as the men got off work and came in.

Fearing being recognized if Smoke came in, he lowered his head and walked out of the bar. It had gotten dark and some of the businesses had hung lanterns out to guide their drunken patrons. He barely stepped on the walk of the mercantile across the street when he heard someone call out Heller's name.

Turning instinctively, Bart saw the slave hunter walking up the street, bantering with one of the ladies of the night. The man who called stood in front of the Harpoon. He waved to Smoke and said, "I'll go in and have a drink waiting. If you make a deal with the girlie, I'll drink the damn thing."

Looking up and waving the man away, Smoke continued talking and poking at the girl. When he tried to grab her by the hair, she ducked out of his reach, laughing at him. He stepped up and backhanded her unexpectedly, sending her rolling into the street.

She cowered from him as he stepped forward. For a moment, Bart thought he was going to kick her. Instead, he cursed at her and headed for the bar.

Another man standing beside Bart chuckled at the spectacle. "That Heller don't like a woman to say nothing but yes. She was probably better off with just the cuffing."

Bart tried to make himself small by standing in the doorway of the store. Smoke reached the Harpoon and stopped a moment before stepping in. He looked in the direction of the mercantile. Whether Bart was seen or not, he did not know.

Turning to enter the Harpoon, Smoke yelled, "Where the hell's my drink?"

The big man knew he had taken a chance of being seen by coming to the Harpoon. A man of his size and stature would find it difficult to hide. A sideways glance is often all it took for someone to pick out a familiar form.

Looking up and down the street, Bart searched for a place where he could keep an eye on the Harpoon. He had decided to follow Smoke, or Heller, or whatever the man's real name was, when he left the saloon. He would take him down in the darkness of some convenient alley.

What he would do then? Bart was not sure. But he knew that when the night was over, women wouldn't have to fear the likes of the slave hunter anymore.

He walked along the street away from the livery and Harpoon, looking for a place to watch without being observed. A couple of buildings down, he found a stairway leading to a second floor. There were two empty wooden barrels stored under the stairs. Ducking below the edge, he tipped one of the barrels over and sat on it. The location was well-concealed in the dark and had a full view of the front of the Harpoon.

The night was long and uncomfortable as Bart sat watching for Smoke to come out. From the dark alley, he had a good view of the night sky. It was well after midnight. The activity on the street was dying down.

He had seen women coming up to longshoremen and cowboys, offering favors for a price. Some left together, others moved on looking for a more agreeable customer. There were several fights, all of short duration, with the loser lying unconscious in the street. At least one cowboy was attacked from behind by two young men and had his money stolen. The boys ran up the street, waving their booty and laughing.

The wharf was a dangerous place to drink, yet it drew men because of the excitement offered. For a price, almost any kind of pleasure could be had.

Fighting to keep his eyes open, he knew it was time to get up and move, or soon he would be sleeping, wasting all time spent watching the door. Stepping to the edge of the walk, he looked up and down the street. Bart decided to chance a look into the Harpoon.

Walking across the street, he angled to the corner of the saloon. He moved to the edge of the window. He tried to prevent the lantern light from falling on him. Pushing his hat back, he looked in the window, keeping half his face hidden.

There were four tables occupied by card players. Two ladies wandered around them looking for drink offers, or maybe more from a big winner. Five men were at the bar with two more women. None of the men in the saloon were Smoke. Bart knew that there were some back rooms. It was possible he was in one of them.

Glancing around the street, he saw no sign of the man. Bart then went into the Harpoon and went up to the end of the bar. The same bartender was still on duty, his shirt no longer clean, and his eyes tired.

He came over with a half-smile. "Hope you're not after another free beer."

"I'm surprised you remembered me," Bart replied.

"Maybe wouldn't have," he said. "Heller came in looking for you earlier. Or at least a big man he described that looked like you. Can I get you a beer?"

"Yes. You say he asked about me?"

Bringing the brew, he set it down on the bar. "Told him you had been in and gone. Said he was sorry he missed you."

"I imagine he was. Funny I didn't run into him on the street."

Taking the cloth he had hanging over his shoulder, he began wiping down the bar. "Left by the side door. I figured he was using the shitter. Come to think of it, he didn't come back."

Drinking down the beer, Bart placed a coin on the bar. "I'll see him soon enough."

The man moved down the bar to see if anyone else needed a drink. One of the woman leaned provocatively against the bar and smiled at Bart. Shaking his head at the lady, he left the Harpoon. Not wanting to expose himself in front of the saloon, he also chose the side door.

The alley was dark and muddy, with the strong smell of urine. Evidently, many of the men didn't go too far to relieve themselves. Walking to the street, he stood just in the shadows. He wondered if he was being too careful. There was a good chance that Smoke had left the saloon and planned to stay out of sight.

He must have seen Bart across the street after hitting the girl. He might have believed it was just coincidence that the big man had stopped into the Harpoon. Whatever might be going through Smoke's mind, Bart knew what he had to do.

The plan to take the man at the wharf was

gone. He would have to wait near the Fisher place and take him out there. Feeling uncomfortable exposing himself to the light in the streets, he went down the alley and made his way back to the livery, walking behind the buildings.

Moving quietly was difficult with all the bottles, scrap wood, and other garbage tossed out the back doors. He tripped over one passed out drunk and almost fell headlong, burying one knee in something wet. Finally arriving across the street from the livery, he was relieved to see there were no porch lanterns which would expose him.

The only light came from the crescent moon, peeking in and out of the clouds. In the near darkness he crossed the street to the livery door. Bart peered into the inky darkness and mumbled. "Damn, Cully, a guy could use a lamp burning in here so he didn't kill himself getting into the loft."

Bending to wipe the damp pant leg saved him. The sound of a rifle exploded in his ears as the flash blinded him. Wood chips flew from the door post, spraying the side of his head and back.

Without thinking he dove into the shadows next to the doorway. Slipping the loop off his Colt Dragoon, he strained his eyes to see a target in the darkness, but could only see the dots floating in front of his eyes from the muzzle flash.

Bart stifled a groan as he realized that he had sat heavily against something protruding from the barn wall. Sweat began to run down his face, stinging his eyes. Any minute he expected to feel the agonizing pain of a bullet tearing into his chest.

"Did I get you, big fellow?" a voice from the dark said. "Thought you were pretty smart hiding across the street. I saw you before I clouted the whore. Did that just for your benefit."

He waited for a response, or any sound from Bart. "You know, I can see your leg in the moon light. I'm aiming at your knee cap right now."

Bart looked over. His leg was in plain sight. He knew Smoke was trying to figure out if he had gotten him. If he pulled the leg in, the area he was hiding in would be filled with a hail of bullets. Also, if the shot came, he could fire back at the location of the flash. The thought of being a cripple was better than being dead.

"You know," Smoke continued, "I didn't enjoy your little filly. I took some of the fight out of her for the others. I let them wrestle over her, while I enjoyed your black one. Her man tried to stop me, but a few bites of the whip settled him down."

"After I sell these ones, I might just go back and have a go of your gal. She might like to know what a real man is like."

Bart sat in a rage, listening to the taunting. He knew that Smoke was trying to determine if he was dead or alive. Sitting and hearing about the events was almost too much to bear.

"Who the hell is shooting?"

It was Cully. He pushed the side door open and light spilled from the lantern he carried. Bart saw the surprise on Smoke's face as he looked over. Without hesitation, he leveled the Dragoon and squeezed off two quick shots, slamming the slaver against the horse stall.

Shocked by the gunfire, Cully dropped the lamp and leaped back out of the door. Smoke slid to the floor holding his stomach and groin, his rifle lying on the floor in front of him. Oil leaking from the lamp flared up in the straw.

Bart crossed the open area in two steps and kicked the rifle away from Smoke. Then, grabbing a sack, he began to smother the flames. "Get back in here and help me, Cully!" he barked.

Peeking around the edge of the side door, Cully made sure the gunfight was over before stepping in. He picked up the lantern, blowing out the flames still burning on its outside. With the fire out, Bart turned to the slave hunter. He lay on his side groaning from the pain of his wounds.

"I'll go get the doc," Cully offered.

"This man does not need a doctor. Ain't anything can be done for him. I will take him up the road and bury him proper when he is dead," Bart said.

Cully looked at the pitiful man, clutching his lower stomach and moaning. "Doc could give him some laudanum for the pain."

"Now, Cully," Bart said with cold and piercing eyes, "I know what the man needs. You check on your stock and bring his to me. Then go back to bed. I don't want to repeat myself."

Hurrying around the livery barn, Cully checked on the stock muttering, "It ain't right. It just ain't right."

Soon, he had Smoke's paint and the others standing in front of the livery. Meanwhile, Bart saddled the buckskin while keeping an eye on Smoke. Cully came into the barn, breathing hard from frantically preparing the horses.

"All set, mister. I put his saddle on the gray. He still owes $3.00 on the bill."

Bart rolled the wounded man over and

searched the pockets of his blood soaked trousers. He fished out several coins. Tossing a Half Eagle to the man, he said, "I'll need a shovel, and you can keep the extra for your trouble."

Cully stood wide-eyed as he watched Bart pick Smoke up and put him belly down over the gray's saddle. Reaching under the horse, he looped a piece of rawhide string around the man's wrist and tied the other end to his boot. Stepping back, Bart realized that this was the second time he had tied the man over a saddle.

Securing the extra rifle and a short shovel to his bedroll, he swung onto the buckskin. Hanging on to the three lead ropes, he looked back at Cully. "I believe we are square with the money. I paid you for two nights in the loft. I doubt we will see each other again."

Touching the horse with his heels, he left the livery at a trot, the wounded man bouncing on the saddle, crying in pain.

He stopped in a grove of trees next to a creek. It was just under a mile from the Fisher place. He lowered Smoke to the ground. It appeared he was unconscious. Stripping the saddles from the horses, he put them out on picket ropes. He carried the bloody saddle to the side of the creek to rinse it off.

Returning, he saw Smoke had moved. "Damn, I hate it when you can't trust a dying man to stay put."

He found him curled up behind one of the trees. "Need help where you're going?" Bart asked.

"You son-of-a-bitch," Smoke said in a raspy voice. "Why don't you just shoot me and get it over with."

"I shot you all I am going to. Now it is up to you to die, however long it takes."

"Gimme a gun. Let me finish it," he begged.

Bart grabbed him by the collar and dragged him back to the spot he planned to camp. "I'll get a fire going and let you see how badly you're hurt." For the first time, he had noticed how the man's legs twisted and turned unnaturally. More than likely the groin shot had broken his hip.

With the fire going, Bart put water on for coffee. It was only a few hours before daylight. He would get no sleep tonight. When the sun came up, he had to deal with the folks at the Fisher place.

"Give me a drink of water," Smoke whispered.

"You got a whole damn creek beside you. You dragged yourself back of the trees. You can get yourself to the water," Bart told him.

Walking away from the wounded man, he could hear him struggling to get to the water. Much of the pleasure of seeing the cruel Smoke reduced to a groveling mess had worn off. It wasn't in him to shoot the defenseless man.

Bart sat watching the coffee water heat. Cully's words kept going through his mind. "Damn you, Smoke. Hold up, I'll get you some water."

He heard splashing coming from the creek. Smoke had dragged himself to the edge and slipped half-way in. He was struggling to turn himself over. Weak from blood loss, his attempts were feeble.

Hurrying to the creek, Bart turned him over and held his head up. Coughing and gasping, the man struggled to breath. Holding the wounded man, he felt him go limp, the last of his breath wheezing out. The big man stood up and looked at the still form.

"I guess you finished what I started. May you burn in hell a long time. No doubt you will be waiting when I get there." Grabbing the man's ankles, he pulled him out of the water. The bones in the broken hips ground together, sounding a little like pulling off a leg of a chicken.

The coffee water was ready. Dumping a measure of grounds in, he was soon sitting with a cup of the brew. Bart sat staring at the broken man. He would never know all the untold cruelty that Smoke had done. He knew that the man deserved to be left to be scavenged by animals, but it would be foolish to leave the body to be found. Soon the law would be chasing him. Finishing his coffee, Bart took up a short shovel and began to dig.

He was tossing the last of the dirt onto the unmarked grave when the sun came up. Pitching the shovel into the trees, he went to the creek to wash up. While going through Smoke's pockets, he'd found the forged ownership papers for Joshua's family. They were made out to the name of Jedidiah Heller.

Smoke had just over $100 on him. Bart felt it would be fitting if the money went to pay for the expenses at the Fisher place. Anything left over he would give to Joshua. Saddling up the buckskin and putting the other one on the mustang, he rode away from the grove knowing that justice had been done.

The Fisher place was busy. He passed carts and wagons along the road, loaded with slaves for the auction. He could hear shouts and the clanging of cage doors coming from the back. The front porch was empty of any guards.

Tying the four horses to the hitching rail, he walked around the building. The old woman stood on the back steps, holding the hanky to her nose. The two guards he had seen before were opening cages and herding the slaves out as the owners produced papers.

The ill man still lay in the bottom of his cage. Bart walked to the cage that Joshua and his family was in. They stood there expectantly, watching his approach.

"Hold up there, money is owed on these ones," one of the guards said, stepping in front of Bart. Grabbing the man by the shirt, Bart slammed him against the cage.

"Don't you be getting between me and my property," he snarled.

The high-pitched voice of the woman cut through the air. "You and Jedidiah owe $40 for the special care of your blacks."

The angry guard regained his control and snapped, "Where's Heller? I need to see the paper on these blacks."

Pulling the documents of ownership out, Bart handed them to the guard. "He sent me up to get them. He had a big night and is having trouble getting around."

Then, placing the required money into the guard's hand, he took the papers back and watched as the cage was opened. Roughly, the man pulled Joshua's family out of the cage. Their leg irons rattled and cut into their ankles as they stumbled out.

"You put a mark on those blacks and I'll take the lost value out of your hide," Bart threatened.

Stomping away, the guard brought the money to the woman. Bart was left with Joshua's family. "Boss Bart, you got to help the old man in the cage over there," Joshua whispered.

"He is old and sick. Close to dying," Bart said.

"His only problem is he's starving. The man

that brought him here a week ago ain't come back. Without money in hand, they quit feeding him."

"I don't have papers on him. They won't give him to me."

"Jess ask, Boss Bart. Jess ask the old woman," Joshua pleaded.

Bringing the family to the front of the building, he told Joshua to get them on the horses. He walked up on the porch and pounded on the door. One of the guards came hurrying around the side of the building carrying a scattergun.

He came face-to-face with the business end of Bart's Colt Dragoon. "Take it easy, my friend. I just want to talk to the old woman."

"Mrs. Heller doesn't meet the likes of you in the house. Maybe you should send her nephew," the guard said, staring at the revolver.

Putting the gun away, Bart stepped away from the door. He now realized that the old woman and Smoke were kin. He was sure they would be in trouble if they didn't get out of the Galveston area in a hurry.

"You got an old man back there. I could use him to take care of light work around my farm while he gets his strength back. After he is healthy, he will be worth a few dollars. If you could check with her, I'd like to know what is owed to get him out."

Looking at Bart like he had lost his senses, the guard walked back around the house. The big man knew that he should get on his horse and ride hard and fast away from the Fisher place. At any time word could come from Galveston that Smoke had been shot.

Moving down the steps, he went back to the horses. He slipped his money belt from around his waist and handed it to Joshua. "Take this belt. It has some money. If something happens to me use it to try and go north."

He reached into his saddle bag and pulled out the dress and shirt. He handed them to Sara. He then took out the peppermint sticks and handed them to Nate and Mary. The children took them and stared with fear-filled eyes at Bart.

"Now go a bit up the road and I will be right along."

He watched as the family rode away. The lash marks on Joshua were healing, but would leave lasting scars. The swelling had gone down on Sara's eye. She looked back at him a look of determination. It gave him confidence that if he couldn't make it back to them, Joshua and Sara would make it north.

Deciding not to wait for the guard to come back, Bart walked around the house. He found him talking to the old woman. She was saying something to the guard and pointing at Bart.

As he watched, he heard the cocking of a scattergun behind him. "Where did your blacks go off to? Are you trying to cheat Jedidiah out of his share?"

The skin on Bart's back crawled, fearing a load of buckshot. "I told them to go up the road and wait for me. They are scared of Smoke. I promised them they would be sold as a family if they minded what I asked."

"And you trust the blacks?" he said, tapping Bart's back with the gun barrel.

Chuckling, the big man answered, "You know how stupid they are. They're willing to believe anything. I don't give a damn how Smoke sells them."

Bart hoped using the name he was familiar with would help convince the shotgun toting guard. He saw that the other was walking back. Mrs. Heller must have given him a price for the sickly slave.

"I would appreciate you taking that gun out of my back. If you slip in this shit, you just might blow my head off," Bart requested.

The gun moved away and he heard the hammers being put back on half-cock. The guard coming at him was carrying a piece of paper.

"Mrs. Heller was owed $70 for the man. She heard that the owner was killed on the wharf. He's yours if you got the money."

He thought of the money belt he had given Joshua. He only had $62 left from Smoke. He didn't dare stay and haggle. It was time to get out of here. "Too much. You haven't even fed him in days. I'll be on my way."

"What you figure he's worth?" The guard countered.

Suddenly, the last thing he wanted was to have to take the old man with him. He decided to offer a very low price and be on his way. "He ain't worth $30, in fact he ain't worth the food it would take to bring him back. No thanks, I got to catch up to my blacks."

Turning to leave, the guard called out, "$20 and he's yours. Just take him now."

He realized that during the deal making, the two guards had put themselves between him and his way out. He reached into his pocket and took out four half eagles. Handing them to the guard, he was given paper on the man.

Two things instantly struck Bart. He was now a slave owner, and he wasn't sure the man he bought was even alive. The guard that he had given money to hurried, bring it to Mrs. Heller. The other, cradling the shotgun, unlocked the cage and dragged the old man out. With a shaky hand, the slave tried to shield his face to protect himself.

Lifting the man up, Bart half-carried and half-dragged him toward the buckskin. The sneering guard walked alongside. "You sure got yourself a prize there," he scoffed.

Ignoring the comment, Bart picked up the foul-smelling man, and put him on the saddle. Then, climbing up behind him, he was ready to leave. Looking back, he saw the guard he had negotiated with bringing a horse around.

"Thought I would ride with you and say hello to Jedidiah. Make sure his horses and blacks get back to him." Mounting, he positioned himself behind the buckskin.

The look on Bart's face was one of confusion with the new development. The guard misread the look and said, "The old one doesn't let us call him Smoke."

Bart knew that he would have little choice but to kill this guard. It went against his grain to kill a man who had done nothing to him. He searched his brain for a way out and none came. He decided to make his move as soon as the Fisher place was out of sight. Then there was a shout.

It was the guard with the shotgun. "Damn you, Kelly! Get back here and help me get the cages ready for tonight's blacks. We got to hurry. Mrs. Heller wants to go to the auction and see her nephew."

Bart kept on riding as he heard the guard turn back, hollering obscenities at the other.

CHAPTER FOURTEEN

Riding with his foul-smelling man cradled in front of him, Bart felt exposed to the dangers behind. He followed the trail toward Joshua and his family. He wanted to let the buckskin gallop and put distance between himself and Mrs. Heller. Carrying the man prevented that.

He expected the man in front of him to die any moment. He rode wide of Wil's cabin. He didn't want to have to explain the half-dead black in front of him. A mile beyond the cabin, Bart stopped and lowered the old man to the ground. He gave him some water and wished that he had time to make a broth to feed him.

He seemed to be more alert, and grabbed Bart's arm. "Massa, ah is Samuel. Thanky for takin' me with you."

Seeing the fire in the man's eyes, he said, "Well, Samuel, you just might make it."

Soaking some hard bread in a cup of water, he placed softened pieces in the man's mouth. He slowly chewed on the bread. Bart took some extra time to give Samuel a chance to eat a little more. Bart knew that it was not good to feed a starving man too much at once.

Samuel was able to stand next to the buckskin

as Bart swung into the saddle. Gripping the black man's arm, he was able to get him seated behind this time. That would make travel easier, and more importantly, move the smell behind him.

"You best hang on tight. You fall off and I just might leave you," Bart warned.

The family's tracks were easy for Bart to follow. Joshua had kept to the trails just off the road. It had been safer, preventing them from meeting any riders. The thorny brush had torn at their legs as they rode.

He found them a half-hour from Wil's cabin. The family had set up a simple camp. They were cooking some wild greens in a dented pot. Joshua hurried to help Samuel down. He was wearing the new shirt and Sara had the clean dress on. Their ankle chains had been removed. Bart didn't know how they'd done it, but was glad that they were gone.

"Joshua, can you and Sara get Samuel here cleaned up and get some of that soup in him?" Digging in his saddlebags, he pulled out a spare pair of trousers. Tossing them to Sara, he said, "Have him put these on until his clothes are cleaned."

He kept an eye on the road while the family ate and made ready to keep traveling. Bart was pleased to see the children playing near the water. He would never understand how abuses could be heaped on the blacks and once away from the shadow of the abuser, they could overcome them so quickly.

It took a week to get back to the ranch. Memories of the violence to someone he had loved were strong on the place and he was anxious to leave. The day after arriving, he went to Wolfgang's and asked him to watch over Joshua and his family. He also needed him to vouch that the slaves were his and he had the authority to give them their freedom.

He had two copies of the documents made, one copy each for Joshua's family and Samuel, making them free slaves. The second set was to be held by Wolfgang in case someone tried to take them again. He told Wolfgang about killing Smoke. He also warned him of Mrs. Heller in the event she or someone working for her showed up.

With the final document, he made Joshua responsible for running operations on the ranch. Samuel, who had regained his strength and health with proper food, was put on as a hired man. With these items finished, he made ready to head for Santa Fe to find Jonny.

It was late October. Temperatures were still comfortable in Waco. With the buckskin saddled and his saddlebags filled with food enough for two weeks, he met with Joshua.

"You're in charge of the place until I return." Bart handed a small leather bag to Joshua. "In the bag is the rest of Smoke's money and some additional that I added. I'm taking his horse so it can't be traced to the ranch. You will have the gray and mustang. You may want to use some of the money to purchase a couple more horses. Use the cattle as you see fit. You can plant whatever you think will be a good cash crop."

Joshua looked toward the half-built ranch house. "Boss Bart, you want me to keep working on your home?"

"Only if you want to move into it," Bart replied.

Climbing on the buckskin's saddle, he took the lead rope of the paint from Joshua. He saw Samuel hurrying toward him with his rolling gait.

"Massa Bart. I wants to thank you for making me free. I will work hard on your place."

"Thank you, Samuel, and it's Boss Bart. You are a free man, remember?" Bart said, turning the buckskin and heading to find Jonny Tucker.

* * *

Bart knew that it would take most of a month to get to Santa Fe. He also knew that while the war with Mexico was over, he would be traveling through some of the disputed land. The Brazos River would take him over half of the way. A series of dusty roads or trails wound along its basin.

There were few towns of any size. Most villages were occupied by Mexicans, their houses built of adobe. There would be a center for celebrations and a church or other place of worship. The streets were narrow, best suited for carts or pack mules.

Bart rotated between riding the buckskin and the paint. He was making good time, spending most hours from sunrise to sunset, in the saddle. One day was lost when he saw a group of well-armed men who appeared to be tracking someone.

To avoid them, he took a cut he found in the ledge running along the Brazos and rode a couple of miles into it until he came upon an abandoned stone house. The thatched roof had caved in years before. There was a spring flowing out of the sandstone wall.

Exhausted from days of riding, he spent most of a day and night resting behind the walls of the house. There was good grass off the watershed of the spring. The horses spent the time grazing and drinking from the spring.

Bart awoke feeling a little stiff, but much more rested, on the second day. He had been on the trail for 10 days and was over half the way to Santa Fe. Using both horses, he was making almost 50 miles each day. At this rate, it would take just over a week to be in New Mexico. He would have to be on the constant alert for Comanches, or Comancheros. They would kill him for his horses and guns without a thought.

His supplies were running low. He sliced the last of his salt pork into the frying pan and mixed up some sourdough bread to fry in the grease. He had water heating for coffee. There was enough left for one more weak pot after this one.

He had found few places along the way that carried coffee or flour. Beans would soon be his main meal. Bart didn't have time to hunt for game. The only fresh meat he'd had on the trip was rattlesnake.

He drank the coffee while dunking the fried bread into the cup between sips. The crisp, salty pork was eaten using his knife to skewer pieces out of the pan. Wrapping some fried bread and pork in a cloth, he put them into his saddlebag to be eaten later in the day.

The horses snorted and stomped as he walked toward the spring. He put the saddle on the buckskin and the saddlebags on the paint using a rigging he had gotten in one of the small villages. Sharing the weight made travel a bit easier for the two horses.

Arriving back at the Brazos River, he took care to watch for trouble. Seeing that the area was empty, he moved out at a trot. Soon he would be leaving the river basin and begin climbing. The trail would wind between rock structures and valleys cut by ancient rivers. Blowing sand continued to carve the rock into various shapes.

Bart rode into a village with a cool, inviting cantina. He figured that it was only a few days before he reached Santa Fe. He needed to resupply. For several days he had been living on nopales cactus and the occasional rattlesnake. In a trade with a farmer, he got some beans. He would put the beans on to cook in the evening and they would be done in the morning.

Leaving his horses with a man who stabled animals, he paid him to give them a good rubdown and extra corn. He was looking forward to a hot meal made by someone else. It was just starting to get dark and the cantina was lit by two lanterns. A young Mexican girl brought him some type of sweet drink. It was followed by a platter of warm corn tortillas and clay bowls of chopped greens, peppers, beans, and a meat that he guessed was chicken.

An old Mexican ran the cantina and told him that there was a room he could rent for the night. Bart asked him if he had seen any Americans in the past couple of weeks. He described Tucker and Pascal. The man rubbed his chin and nodded.

"These men you tell me about, they came this way maybe a week ago. The man in skins tried to hurt my nieta. The younger one stopped him and when they left, they had angry words."

"You were lucky," Bart said, understanding that he was talking about the girl who had brought his food. "The man has hurt many women."

"They stole a horse from a farm not far from here. The one they left behind was hurt and had to be put down."

Bart paid for his meal and the room. He turned

141

in right after eating. This was the fourth place that had seen the men he was looking for. He was pleased that each time he had made up time following them. Lying on the straw mat on the floor, he fell asleep almost immediately. He dreamed of Millie, that she was calling him and he couldn't find her. He wanted to run, but his legs didn't want to move.

Then there was someone shouting in his dream. He awoke, but the shouts didn't stop. It was coming from the main room. He heard the crash of a table. The girl screamed.

Bart had his Colt Dragoon lying on the floor next to his mat. Picking it up, he moved quickly to the doorway. He saw the girl leaning over her grandfather lying on the floor next to the bar. Two men stood over her, laughing and sharing a jug of tequila. One was carrying an older revolver, and both had rifles similar to those used by the Mexican Army.

Bart stepped into the room and shouted at the men in Spanish. "What are you beaters of old men doing?"

They dropped the jug and turned, grabbing their rifles leaning against the bar. They attempted to bring them to bear on the big man. He leveled the Dragoon and it bucked twice, putting well-placed shots into each of the men. The impact of the bullets knocked them back against the bar.

One of the men slid down the bar to the floor, his head hanging to one side. The other caught himself on the edge of the bar. Blood was spreading across his shirt. He tried to raise the rifle to fire. Bart squeezed off another shot, putting a bullet into the man's chest. He fell forward and the rifle discharged, the bullet ricocheting off the far wall.

Smoke from the weapons hung thickly in the enclosed room, burning Bart's eyes. The girl crouched near her grandfather, holding her hands over her ears. He shoved the rifles away from the men as he walked past. Bart helped the girl up before kneeling to check on her father. He had a severe gash on his temple.

The girl screamed as she looked past him. Bart pushed her aside as he twisted around, bringing the Colt Dragoon around. The man who had slid to the floor was not dead and had drawn a revolver. Fire belched from its barrel, the bullet tearing through Bart's shirt, cutting into his ribcage. Instinctively, he returned fire, hitting the sitting man in the throat.

Continuing to spin, Bart rolled across the floor, unable to catch his breath. Lying on his stomach, he stared at the man, who was clutching his neck, blood running out between his fingers and out of his mouth. The revolver lay on the floor, forgotten in the throes of his death struggle.

Bart tried to get up. The pain from a broken rib shot through his body, causing him to collapse back to the floor, moaning. After a moment, he slowly got into sitting position. He could feel blood running down his side.

The girl ignored the big man who had come to her rescue and was busy staunching the blood coming from her grandfather's cut. Bart put the Colt Dragoon back into his holster, confident that both of the men were now dead.

The old man got up, assuring his granddaughter that he was okay. Looking at the two dead men and then Bart, he realized that the big man had been wounded during the exchange. He told the girl, Noemi, to get him rags and hot water. Forgetting his own injury, he knelt next to Bart and began to remove the shirt to inspect the wound.

Some villagers came into the cantina, having heard the gunfire. They stopped short, looking at the bodies.

"Quickly, drag them out back and move their horses to the stable," the old man instructed. He then turned back to helping Bart.

There was an ugly, red gash along his side caused by the gunshot. The bullet had fractured a rib, making breathing painful. The old man helped him into a chair. Bart sat with sweat running down his face, even though the room was cool.

Taking shallow breaths and fighting to stifle moans, he sat as the man cleaned and bandaged the wound. He wrapped lengths of cloth around Bart's chest to support the broken rib.

"I am sorry that you were shot helping my granddaughter and me," the old man said in Spanish.

Answering, Bart said, "I was foolish not to take the revolver from the man sitting against the bar. It was a mistake that almost got me killed."

"I am Jose Diaz. My granddaughter Noemi and I run this cantina. The men you killed were Comancheros. There are those in the village that will tell them what happened here. Others will come to seek revenge. They will kill me and have their way with the girl and then kill or sell her."

"I didn't mean to bring you trouble," Bart said, gasping as he took a too deep a breath.

"Trouble was already here. They would have taken Noemi with them. Me, they would probably have left. You saved us from a fate worse than death."

The girl came back out with a steaming cup of

some type of tea. She set it on the table next to Bart. Jose pointed at the brew. "You drink this and it will help with the pain."

Sipping the bitter tea, Bart sat, beginning to feel tired. The pain was somewhat better. With the help of the old man, he went back to his room and lay on the mat. He lay in semi-sleep, knowing that he should reload the Dragoon. It was the last thing he remembered before sleep overtook him.

Bart awoke, feeling alarmed. He stared at the roof beams supporting the adobe bricks. He was unsure of where he was. Trying to sit up caused severe pain to shoot through his upper body, quickly bringing back memories of the night before. He collapsed back onto the mat and struggled to breathe over the burning.

"You are awake," Jose said. "I have something for you to eat, before we leave."

"Leave . . . us?" Bart asked, trying to clear the cobwebs from his brain. He then groaned from trying to turn toward the man.

"Let me help you get up. I would give you more drink for the pain, but it would make staying awake very hard."

Sweating from the exertion of just getting up, Bart rested at a table in the cantina. He drew the Colt Dragoon to reload and found that it had been done for him. He looked up at Jose.

"I wanted you to be ready in case others came. Eat now, so we can leave."

The man had a bandage around his head. His right eye was swollen and black and blue. Yet he was smiling and quickly moving pots, dishes, and other items of his trade out of the cantina.

Noemi had brought Bart a plate of tortillas filled with scrambled eggs. It was not often that he enjoyed eggs. Despite the pain caused by breathing and swallowing, he couldn't pass up such a meal.

Before they left, she brought a pan of warm water and clean bandages. Removing the bloody shirt and the bandages from last night, she carefully cleaned the wound. The flesh around the gash had turned green and blue from the bruising blow. With the wound bandaged, she handed him his extra shirt.

It was early and the air outside was cool. Bart found his horse saddled and his saddlebags on the paint. Jose had two burros packed with a few personal items and as much as they could carry from the cantina. He and Noemi were going to ride the Comancheros' horses.

Any jarring or bumps caused pain and made breathing difficult. He knew that time would be lost riding the rest of the way to Santa Fe. He looked at the burros and shook his head. He knew that they wouldn't move very fast.

Mounting with difficulty, he led the group out of the sleeping village. Bart had to keep the buckskin at a walk to prevent severe pain. Jose rode up beside him, letting Noemi lead the two burros.

"If we get away from the Comancheros, I have a brother in Santa Fe. I will work with him at his cantina."

Bart looked over at the old man. "Will you ever be able to return to your village?"

"No, the friends of the two you killed will find out it happened at my cantina. They will try and find me, and you too. I just pray they do not hurt others for what was done. Many will flee to the hills, just in case."

The morning sun blazed above them by midday. The coolness of the morning was long gone. Sweat stung Bart's eyes and the constant rocking of the horse had his side aching. They came to a pool of water next to a canyon wall. Bart needed help getting off the buckskin.

Sitting against a boulder with his hands on his knees, he fought to catch his breath. He would give anything to be able to breathe deeply. Noemi brought him tortillas wrapped around some greens and some type of meat.

After the pain subsided enough, he drank from his canteen before trying the food. He took a bite and chewed a couple times before the heat of the peppers hit him. Needing something to eat, he finished the spicy meal. Several sips of water did little to stop the burning after the food.

Seeing the sweat stand out on Bart's forehead, Jose chuckled. "Noemi likes to put in many peppers. I will ask her to put fewer in your food."

Smiling at the old Mexican, Bart said, "I would appreciate less heat in the food. Your Noemi is a very good cook."

Soon, they were back on the trail, Bart now riding the paint. He favored the broken rib, accepting the ache as something he would have to live with. He hoped that there was more of the bitter tea for him that night.

Scratching his itchy beard, he looked back at Noemi. She was a good girl. Much of the work on the trip was done by her. She didn't complain, and he noticed that she did not smile. Jose had told him that her parents had been killed by Comancheros while she hid in some rocks away from the house.

It was a savage way for a young woman to start her life. Bart knew that the danger of the Comancheros, as well as Apaches and Comanches, was a constant cloud over people of the New Mexico territory.

The afternoon was late when Jose pulled alongside Bart and motioned to their back trail. There was dust from several riders on the horizon. They had been riding on a well-traveled trail to help hide their passing. All familiar with the desert knew that travelers had to go from waterhole to waterhole.

Bart hoped that he would be able to carry his own if a fight developed. The wound was on his right side. He could fire almost as well with the left hand. That would help, but he had to fire the Hawken on the right. He was not sure he could do that.

Jose moved into the lead and took them up a cut that was smooth rock, leaving very little evidence of their passing. He stopped behind a series of boulders that would give them a chance of defending themselves.

Bart tried to dismount, but each time he tried to do so the pain stopped him. A feeling of helplessness washed over him. Jose helped him down. The girl had already moved their horses and the burros deeper into the boulders. She returned with the two rifles taken from the dead Comancheros.

Leaving the weapons, she took Bart's horses to put them with the others. Bart got behind a boulder that would give him good shooting angles down the cut. Jose pulled the old revolver out of his belt and set a rifle alongside. Noemi set up a safe place to reload their rifles. Seeing their preparation gave Bart hope that they might just get out of this alive.

The hot afternoon sun burned the three as they waited. The sound of the riders was growing louder. An occasional shout could be heard. They sat with sweat trickling under their clothes as they listened. They hardly dared to breathe as the horsemen came closer.

Then the drum of the horses' pounding hooves sounded like they were right in the cut. Bart tried to find a comfortable position to fire the Hawken. He prayed that after firing the rifle, he would be able to breathe and empty the Colt Dragoon at the Comancheros.

Expecting to see the Comancheros to come around the cut any moment, they crouched behind the boulders. Bart blinked rapidly, trying to clear the stinging sweat from his eyes. The weapons were hot from the burning sun.

Then the sound of the running horses began to lessen. The riders had passed the cut and continued. Bart gasped for air, sending pain through his side. He realized that he had been holding his breath.

"Thank God," Jose said, "they went by."

Bart said, "Amen."

He looked over at Noemi. She had tears of relief running down her cheeks. Without hesitation, the girl began to bring the powder and bullets back to the pack animals. Bart estimated her age to be 13 to 15. The young Mexican boy who married her would be a very lucky man.

The thought brought back the feeling of loss and regret that he and Millie would never be man and wife. The emptiness was soon replaced with the anger toward the men who had attacked her. Knowing that he was only a couple of days from one of the men rekindled the rage that had been dampened by the weeks on the trail.

Jose was watching Bart. He said, "A cloud had just come over your face. There is an anger that is not about the Comancheros."

Bart looked at the somber face of the old Mexican. "There are men I am looking for. Men that hurt someone I loved. They stole the life I hoped to make. One of them may be in Santa Fe. His day of reckoning is getting close."

"Nowhere is it written that the course of life is only as we want it. God only knows what is to come. The Comancheros killed my son and his wife. They died terribly at their cruel hands. I only thought of somehow hurting them more than the pain I felt. It would not bring my son back."

Looking toward Noemi, he continued. "Today, she wanted the Comancheros to come down the cut. She wanted to see them fall and die. Noemi would have sacrificed her life to see some of their bloodshed. She cries at night for a life that was lost. I pray for her to accept what has happened and look for joy in the future."

Shaking his head, he looked at Bart with tears in his eyes. "If you find a way to shed the cloak of pain, tell me so I can help her."

Not knowing what to say to the man, Bart walked back to get his horses. He realized that the tears on her cheeks were not of relief, but rather disappointment that the Comancheros had gone past.

With the gear stowed and the three of them in the saddle, Jose said, "We will need to come into Santa Fe from the south. That way we avoid meeting the men coming back."

Without waiting for an answer, he led the way along the cut. It opened into a wide valley with the Pecos River winding through. It was refreshing to see the green of the valley and hillsides after traveling through the dry country.

Each night, Noemi made the bitter tea for Bart. It relieved the pain and helped him sleep. She would change the bandage and apply a poultice before putting the new bandage on. They kept their fire small and made sure it was out before dark. They avoided other travelers, not wanting their location being spoken of when strangers were making conversation.

Bart found himself looking forward to the tea each night. It worried him that he wanted it more for the relaxing effect than for the pain. He was thankful that his breathing was normal again. Jose said that it would only be another day before they arrived in Santa Fe.

Bart remained concerned that he was in the territory that had Comancheros and Apaches. The sooner he took care of Jonny and headed north, the safer he would be.

The next morning, Jose had the horses ready and Noemi was busy cleaning up from the morning meal. The old Mexican walked over to Bart. "Noemi and I will go on from here alone. It is better if we come in at different times. I will release the Comancheros' horses. We will walk leading the burros."

"Señor Diaz, I want to thank you for the help you gave me. If I find that answer, I will let you know."

With a quick smile, Jose said, "If you need to find me, my brother is Benito. Everyone will know his cantina."

Climbing into his saddle, Bart waved to the two Mexicans. Turning the paint, he led the buckskin and set off at a trot. He would miss the tea, but at least the rib pain was tolerable now. He looked north, hoping that his stay in Santa Fe would be short.

CHAPTER FIFTEEN

Santa Fe was a small, unimpressive town. The scattering of adobe buildings on narrow streets made the town look busier than it was. There were several stands set up in the square selling fruits, vegetables, and assorted peppers. One man was busy making and repairing shoes, another had cages with chickens. The smell of cooking filled the air from several stands offering various things wrapped in corn tortillas.

It was late morning, and soon the market place would be empty as the merchants and shoppers went home for their siesta. Bart bought some melon and a small basket lined with a maize husk. It had tortillas, beans, and seasoned meat they called barbacoa. He set the food carefully into one of his saddlebags to be eaten later.

He stayed away from Jose's brother's place, trying to avoid bringing attention to it. Talking with the vendors at the market, he claimed that he was looking for an American friend named Jonny Tucker. He used the same description that he had been given in Waco.

He was almost giving up for the day when two vaqueros enjoying wedges of melon took notice of his questions. They told him they had seen the man. He was working on a horse ranch just north of Santa Fe.

Bart's stomach burned. He had not expected to locate the man so quickly. The realization that he was close to finding the second man made the hair on the back of his neck stand.

He caught his reflection in a water trough. The face peering back was that of a stranger. His whiskers had grown into a scruffy beard. His hair hung over half of his ears. Bart decided that after meeting Jonny he would get a bath, haircut, and shave. He figured that even the best man with a gun can be killed by a lucky shot from a greenhorn. No sense in spending money for something that he might not need after the fight.

That night he slept just outside of town. Full from his market shopping, he rolled up in his blankets and stared into the star-filled skies. He had found it awkward changing his own bandage. The wound was not deep, but it was slow to heal. The rib would take time to mend. He had to take care not to bump the right side.

Bart looked at the rising moon. It revealed large, cottony clouds in the sky. The cool, night breeze was coming down from the north, announcing the winter which was just ahead. Rolling to his left side, he pulled the blanket up to his chin and sleep soon overtook him.

The morning was crisp and cold. Bart huddled over his small fire waiting for the water to come to a boil. He had found coffee beans in the Santa Fe market. He was looking forward to the morning brew. The horses snorted and kicked up clods of dirt, feeling refreshed in the bright morning.

Bart fired and reloaded his rifle and revolver,

not wanting any chance of misfires. He had used the left hand shooting the Colt Dragoon and felt good about his hits. He honed the edge of his knife.

He felt none of the anger he had expected. There was just a cold feeling inside. Bart wondered if he hadn't become as removed as a hangman. Methodically, he readied the horses and stowed his gear. He double-checked the cinch on the buckskin, unable to remember if he had done so.

Bart had been in many gunfights. In all cases, his firing had been in response to being challenged or attacked first. This was the first time that he was riding out to kill a man. He wouldn't say that he was scared, for he didn't fear dying. He worried that he would be stopped before getting to all the men he hunted.

Climbing into the saddle, he rode toward the ranch. One of the sellers at the market had given him directions. The Valdez ranch was less than five miles away. Before noon, Jonny Tucker would answer for what had been done to Millie.

As he rode, he pulled and settled the Colt Dragoon several times, taking care to keep the loop off the hammer. He looked at the Hawken. It was unlikely that he would need it. He had no intention of killing the man from a distance.

He began to see horses from the ranch. He even saw several longhorns that probably belonged to the Valdez ranch. He passed some vaqueros, who told him Jonny was rounding up horses toward the west. They pointed to a low plateau.

Thanking them, he turned his horse in the direction of the high ground. He thought of Millie as he rode. Would she support what he was doing? He doubted that she would want him to kill these men.

Well, maybe the trapper. But Jonny and even the slave hunter had done little to her.

He was almost ready to head for the Valdez headquarters when he saw two riders pushing some horses. As he rode closer, he could see that one man was short and heavyset. The other was a thin, lanky rider. He rode toward the men. Some of the horses cut away to the left and the stocky man rode hard after them to turn the animals back.

The lanky man stopped upon seeing Bart. He took off his hat and waved him over. Urging the buckskin into a fast trot and the paint running behind, Bart quickly closed the distance between the two.

"Can I help you, mister?" the lanky man called out.

"Are you Jonny Tucker?" Bart asked.

"You found him. What can I do for you?"

Suddenly, Jonny saw the paint Bart was leading. He stopped his horse and stared wide-eyed at Bart.

"My name's Bart Nevell. I lived with Millie."

"She okay?" he asked. "She is okay, ain't she?"

Anger began to creep into Bart's body. "No, she ain't okay. She is dead. You boys killed her."

Jonny's jaw dropped. "You got to understand, I didn't mean for that to happen. It got out of hand. I couldn't control Bruno."

"Your loop is on your gun," Bart said. "I'll let you take it off."

Looking around, Jonny said, "I don't want to hurt the horses. Let's step away and do this."

He knew that the man was trying to buy time for his friend to come back from turning the horses in. Or, maybe, he would draw his gun while dismounting and use the grulla as a shield.

"I'll give you that, Jonny. Just take care getting off," Bart warned.

Both men stepped away from the animals and Bart looked into the frightened eyes of the young cowboy.

Jonny continued to try and reason with Bart. "Let's don't do this, mister. I'll go back with you to Waco and you can turn me in to the law. I'll even help you get Pascal up in Colorado, and take him back. I don't want to fight you."

Bart stood looking at the man, feeling no compassion. He was remembering Millie's cries of pain as she died.

The look in Jonny's eyes changed from fear to desperation a moment before he drew. His holster was not designed for the fast draw. It was functional and held the revolver in place.

The boy's first grab came up empty, missing getting his fingers around the grip. When he went for his second grab, he watched the fire and smoke come out of Bart's Dragoon. The .44 caliber bullet smashed into his chest, knocking the wind out of him. He pulled the gun from his holster and fell to the brown grass, his unseeing eyes now without emotion.

The stocky rider was coming toward him at a gallop with his rifle in one hand, the reins in the other. Bart holstered the Colt Dragoon and raised both hands above his head. The vaquero stopped short and brought the rifle to bear upon Bart.

Speaking in Spanish, Bart said, "This man, Jonny Tucker, was involved with the death of a woman back in Waco. She was to be my wife. I followed him here and killed him for it. If you would help me get him over his horse, we can take him back to the headquarters and bury him."

Uncertain of what to do, and just a little unsure of his ability to kill the man at the distance even with the rifle, he called out, "Señor, put your guns on the paint and I will take you back to Señor Valdez. He will decide."

He rode, leading the paint ahead of the vaquero. The stocky man led Jonny's horse with the boy's body draped over the saddle.

After a few tense minutes with Señor Valdez, Bart was able to convince the owner that his story was true. Bruno Pascal had spent a couple of nights in the bunkhouse, and when drinking one night he had bragged about teaching a whore some respect down in Texas. The vaquero who had brought him in had heard the story and confirmed the event.

Bart dug a grave not far from the barn, his side burning with every shovel full. The elder Valdez said he would have a marker made for the grave. He felt that the man had paid for his mistakes.

It was late November and the nights were cold. Bart would be traveling over two weeks further north. He would find snow in the mountains, if not before. Señor Valdez told him of a trading post a week north that carried supplies and clothing needed for the winter cold.

After two days of rest as a guest of the Valdez ranch, Bart left to find Bruno Pascal. The wound on his side was still tender, but mostly healed. He now kept a bandage wrapped around his chest, only to prevent the shirt from rubbing the area and giving some support to the rib.

He took a bath and paid a Mexican lady to wash his extra clothes. He decided that it was cold where he was going, so the beard and long hair would help keep him warm. The night before leaving, he was invited to eat in the big house. Bart met the Valdez women. He watched as they fussed putting on the meal. Again he reminded himself, *This was all I asked for. The men I am killing took it away from me.*

CHAPTER SIXTEEN

Bart rode, head lowered, against the north wind. He was riding up the San Luis Valley and the wind had blown all day, every day. Thinking about Jonny's death, he didn't feel any better. Had the young man only been in the wrong place? Should Bart have let him go? He had no answer. He tried to think about Bruno. He deserved killing, as did Smoke. Maybe not Jonny. He had given the boy a chance to draw first. He could feel right about that.

The trail he was following was almost too easy. He realized that the men he searched for were not running. They believed Millie was still alive, and no one would follow them over the beating of a whore. This thought darkened his mood. He forced himself to shake it off and watch the plains around him.

Tumble weeds were rolling across the valley, spreading seeds for next year's growth. The grass was brown, but still offered acceptable grazing for the horses. Slowly, his mood improved and he began to feel excitement over being back on the high desert. It was open and wild. Despite the dryness, game was plentiful. The mountains loomed to the west, offering unexplored peaks and valleys.

Throughout the day, Bart saw herds of buffalo

grazing.   Antelope leaped gracefully away as he approached. There was beauty in the western plains, but there was also loneliness. He had always been with hunters, a wagon train, or with the army. In a matter of days, he knew that he would look forward to meeting someone to talk to.

He planned to stop at the trading post called Fort Pueblo. It was located on the Arkansas River. Because it was a desert area, it got less snow than the northern part of Colorado. He could get clothes and extra blankets for the trip into the mountains.

There would be a good chance that Bruno had stopped there to resupply. He may have talked of where he was headed. Covering such a vast area, one would think that searching for a man would be very difficult. There were only a few places to get supplies. Travel was slow and difficult, so men took the shortest route from one town or trading post to the next.

Bart depended on this during his search. Once Bruno got into the mountains, it would be nearly impossible to search for the valley or stream he had decided to winter on. He might have to spend the winter in the South Platte River area, waiting for the trappers to come down for supplies and sell their catch in the spring.

After the second day at the higher elevation, Bart had to wrap his blanket around himself as he rode to keep warm. He watched a wall of brown go west of him one day, blocking out the view of the mountains. He was thankful that the sandstorm hadn't come further east. He would have had to hold up until the storm passed. There was the danger of losing one or both of his horses.

Fort Pueblo was a few adobe buildings. Most

of the trading was among local residents and tribes in the area. The occasional traveler was always a cause for excitement. The place was hungry for information about the outside. Bart was riding the paint the morning he arrived. It had been too cold to sleep, so he had ridden throughout the night.

The trading post had a fire going. Shivering, Bart walked in and went directly to the fireplace. He turned to warm each side. A large coffee pot sat next to the coals. Seeing the proprietor watching him, he said, "If the coffee is ready, I would pay dearly for a cup."

Before long, Bart was seated, enjoying the warmth of the coffee. A plate of beans and a thick slice of bread were put in front of him. The trading post was run by Peck Anderson. Peck sent a helper out to take care of the horses. They needed rest after traveling a day and night without stopping. After eating the warm meal, Bart crawled onto a stack of hides in the corner of the post and slept for several hours.

The sound of customers talking and laughing with Peck woke the big man. He stiffly crawled out from the hides and sat next to the fire. For the first time, he took a good look around the room.

Along with several stacks of furs and hides, there were traps hanging on the walls. A plank counter was near the door. Behind it were shelves of canned goods. Along another wall were rolls of rope, kegs of flour, beans, and rice. Next to these were stacks of blankets, coats, and other clothing. Bolts of cloth hung from the low ceiling.

His mouth was dry and he needed to go outside and relieve himself. The thought of going into the cold wasn't something he looked forward to. Getting up, he headed for the door.

He heard Peck holler, "You'll find it behind the post."

The boards were cold. Bart sat shivering, wishing the outhouse had a hover rope. After finishing taking care of nature's call, he went to check on his horses. The stable smelled strong of hay and horses. It was warm, so he spent some time rubbing down the animals. He gave each a pail of water and then forked some more hay for them.

He went back into the trading post and found a cup of coffee waiting for him. Peck was putting some canned goods on the rough board shelves. Picking up the coffee, Bart walked over to watch the man work.

"I am looking for a trapper named Bruno Pascal. He would have come this way a few weeks ago, maybe less," Bart said.

Proprietor Anderson frowned. "He came through. Said he was heading for a valley north of Pike's Peak. I believe he mentioned the South Platte River. I was happy to see the one-eyed trouble maker go. He bought a Ute girl from the tribe. Took her with him. He's a mean one, that one is."

"How long ago did he leave?" Bart asked.

"Let's see," Peck thought, "it was about ten days ago when he pulled out. He stole a horse from one of the Mexicans. Beat the man bloody before he left."

"Anyone go after him?"

"No one wanted to face him. The man's a killer."

Bart walked back and refilled his cup. Wandering around the store, he made mental notes of items he would need. After the proprietor was done stocking, he set his cup down and called him over.

"I'm going to need some warm clothing and blankets. I'll be heading into the mountains," Bart said.

Smiling, Peck walked over to a pile of blankets. "I got me some nice Hudson Bay blankets here. I even have a coat made from one that should fit you. Made it for a big fellow that up and died on me."

He handed the colorful woolen coat to Bart. It was made from the Hudson Bay blankets. It would hang below his knees, providing good protection.

Bart selected two blankets, a heavy pair of wool pants designed to go into the top of his boots, two green wool shirts, four pair of woolen stockings, and a woolen hat with flaps that would cover his ears. He also chose a pair of leather choppers with a wool liner.

He picked up a new canvas ground cloth to bundle everything in. It could serve as a makeshift shelter. Settling up with the proprietor, he took the clothing into a back room and changed. His calf-high boots had plenty of room for an extra pair of woolen stockings.

With his winter clothing on, he packed the rest of his belongings into the ground cloth to be carried by his extra horse. The new clothes felt stiff and heavy. If he had to fight, it would slow him down.

Putting on his coat and the wool hat, he went outside. It was near freezing, but he felt very comfortable. He would have to be careful with the heavy clothing. If he began to sweat under the clothes, he would quickly become chilled. He opened the front of the coat and walked around the handful of adobe buildings that made up Fort Pueblo.

Before long he was carrying the coat under his

arm, his long johns and the new woolen shirt providing enough warmth. He passed a man who was chopping wood. He stopped to find out where the horse had been stolen.

The man stopped his work and wiped his forehead with the sleeve of his shirt. "That would be Mario." Pointing to a place with a small corral, he continued, "The trapper took the horse for his woman to ride. Mario tried to stop him and nearly was beaten to death."

Bart walked over to the corral. There were two horses feeding from a pile of hay. Clouds of steam surrounded their heads from their hot breath.

"Can I help you, señor?" a short Mexican asked.

"I was told you had a horse stolen," Bart responded.

The man walked up closer. He had a recent cut from his left ear across his cheek. His nose had been broken and leaned to one side. "Yes, it was my best. A mustang that could run all day. When I tried to stop him he came at me with a knife, cutting, punching and kicking me. I am still not well."

"I will be going after the man and if I can, I will bring the horse back to you."

Looking at the big man in front of him, he shook his head. "I would not if I were you. The man is pure evil. Like a snake, he will strike quickly when you don't expect it."

"Thank you for your concern, but I must go. He caused the death of the woman I was to marry." Nodding goodbye, Bart headed back to the trading post.

The new clothing was warm and would work

well. He planned to leave first thing in the morning. He debated on whether he should leave the paint at Fort Pueblo. By the time he got to the post, he decided that the horse would still speed up his travel. Once in the deeper snow of the mountains, travel would quickly wear down an animal.

Peck was stirring a pot of something that would be tonight's dinner. He looked up as Bart came in. "It will be another hour before the stew is done. I put a jug on the table over there. Pour yourself a drink."

There were two men sitting at the table, enjoying the contents of the jug. As Bart walked up, one of them looked up and laughed.

"What the hell are you suppose to be, all dressed up in a new store-bought outfit, carrying a coat that even an Indian wouldn't wear?"

Smiling back at the man, Bart walked up. Using his left hand, he grabbed the man by the front of his filthy shirt. He held him eye to eye, the fellow's feet swinging above the floor.

"What would wolf pups like you have to talk about, if men like me didn't wear these clothes?"

He tossed the man back into the pile of blankets, the impact knocking his head against the adobe wall. Stunned, the man rolled to the floor and lay still. Turning to the other man, he stared coldly into the concerned eyes.

"Hey, I just stopped in for a drink. The fool you just spoke to was on his own."

Walking around the table, Bart kicked the man's arm out of the way as he went. The man howled and grabbed the arm. He picked up the cup that was still on the counter and went over to the fireplace for a refill.

Peck was cutting some turnips into the stew. "The fellow you spoke to has a problem with his mouth when drinking. He's a good and honest worker, though."

Tasting the coffee, Bart grinned. "Believe I know a man like that."

The proprietor went over to the dazed loud mouth. He helped him up and sat him at the table. "Don't believe the big guy liked your opinion of his clothing. You best shut up and drink."

The next morning was gray and cold. Bart was in the stable, saddling Buck. A day's rest had put the spirit back into the horse. Running his hand down the thick hair on the animal's shoulder, he said, "Too bad I couldn't just grow enough hair to keep warm for the winter." The buckskin bobbed its head. It was ready to go.

He tied the horses in front of the trading post and went in to get the rest of his gear. With clothing to face the cold, he was anxious to get moving.

It was December, and snows had already closed many of the mountain passes. He was about four days from the South Platte River. He planned to search as many valleys and streams as possible before being stopped by the snow.

The wind continued to blow out of the north. Bart rode with his head tilted to the left to protect his face. Small icy flakes were in the air. The new clothing was keeping him comfortable, except for his face.

He carried his midday meal under his coat. The biscuits and cheese he had gotten from the trading post would otherwise be frozen when it was time to eat. His body heat kept it chewable. His long coat draped over the rump of the horse and down the sides of his legs. The warmth of the horse added to his comfort.

Temperatures continued to drop throughout the day. The icy flakes had become hard pellets of snow. The high desert stretched out to the horizon, broken by the occasional grove of trees, or a butte rising above the plain.

Moving to the sway of the walking horse, he dug under his coat and brought out a biscuit. He chewed on the food, and took drinks from the canteen also kept under the coat. The cheese had a pungent, aged smell. The taste was a good contrast to the blander biscuit, satisfying his hunger.

The stinging snow forced Bart to close his eyes. He had to trust the horses to continue the trek north. He felt the wind changing direction. Squinting at the blinding snow, he realized that the animals were turning downwind to put the frigid air at their backs.

Stopping the horses, he looked around for any type of shelter from the coming storm. Bart had been in a blizzard before, and this storm was building to become one. In the distance he could make out a dark shape through the blowing snow. It would disappear, and then reappear, as heavier bands of snow blew by.

With the blowing snow, it was impossible to be sure how far away the shape was. It could be the safety of trees, or just a knoll which would offer no protection. He was riding the paint, and suddenly it refused to move.

Kicking the flanks with his heels, Bart attempted to get the horse to move. After a step or two, it stopped. Frustrated, he climbed stiffly from the horse and took hold of bridle. Crusted snow blown over the horse's face, covering its eyes.

Knocking the frozen snow covering its eyes, he then checked the buckskin. It also was nearly blinded by the snow. This would have happened while trying to ride into the storm. Bart looked for the dark shape. He was unable to see through the snow.

For the first time, Bart began to feel fear that he could truly be in trouble, caught in the open with a blizzard swirling around him. He held the reins and lead rope. Even seeing both of the horses in the storm became impossible. Feeling along the buckskin's back, he attempted to untie the ground cloth pack containing the extra blankets.

The clumsiness of the leather choppers made the task difficult. Pulling one glove off with his teeth, he struggled to loosen the leather straps. His fingers quickly became numb, making it almost impossible.

At last, the bundle came free and slid to the frozen ground. Stepping back to pick it up, Bart felt the ground disappear from under him. The reins and lead rope were pulled from his hand. Sliding a short distance, he clawed with the bare and gloved hand to stop. He came to a jarring stop at the bottom of the slope. Grabbing the chopper from his teeth, he needed to cover the rapidly stiffening hand.

With great effort, he got the mitt back on. Slipping and sliding, he managed to get back up the slope. Crawling around, he searched for the pack. Finding it, he stood, clutching the bundle, and looked for the horses. He was sure that they were only a few feet away, but the blinding snow made them impossible to see.

He opened his mouth to call the buckskin. Snow was driven into it, almost choking him. Turning his back to the wind, he realized that finding the horses was the least of his worries. It was crucial that he find some type of protection from the wind.

Back on his hands and knees, he felt for the edge of the slope. Again he slid down, landing against his face and chest. The sharp crystals of icy snow scraped his nose and cheeks. Stunned for a moment, he rolled his legs to the bottom. Hugging the edge of the slope, he got a little relief from the fury of the wind.

Curled around the bundle at the bottom of the slope, Bart fought to catch his breath. He felt hot under his heavy clothing. He hoped that he didn't begin to sweat. Slowly, the cold began to creep through his clothing. His feet were the first to feel the bite of the winter storm. He knew his face and nose were cut, but they were numb from the cold.

Several years back, Bart had been with an army platoon that had rescued a group of hunters caught in an early winter storm. Half the party had died from the cold. The ones still alive had been severely frost bitten. Ears, noses, fingers, and toes turned black and had to be removed. The pain as the men were warmed had caused them to cry out.

Lying there, Bart knew that he would rather die than survive with severe frostbite. Regaining his wind, he sat with his back to the slope. He was unable to see more than a foot or two around him. The swirling snow made breathing difficult. Squinting, he fought to see.

Opening the pack, he sat on the ground tarp and attempted to wrap it around him. The wind kept tearing it out of his gloved hands. Finally, he had it pulled over his head and secured under his folded legs in front of him. Again, he felt the heat inside his heavy clothing.

Sitting with his legs folded in front, he leaned forward. Removing his leather choppers, he opened the top of his coat. The escaping heat rose, feeling good on his face. After a moment, he pulled the extra blankets he had been sitting on and spread one over his legs and feet. The other, he worked around his back, between the buffeting tarp and his coat. Finally, he had it pulled up to cover the back of his neck and head.

The wind continued to howl around him. Snow continued to work its way under the tarp. He sat for hours, his back and legs aching from the cramped position. Bart feared that moving would allow the tarp to be torn from covering him. He still had the canteen and a biscuit under his coat. He drank sparingly and chewed small bites of the bread at a time.

With the storm raging around him, it would be nearly impossible to relieve himself without the risk of freezing before he could get back under the tarp. That is, if the tarp wasn't ripped from his grasp as he tried to reposition it.

Bart's feet began to tingle, feeling like needles were sticking in them. He knew that they were finally warming. He would rock ahead as blasts of wind hit his back. It was now dark around him. The late afternoon sun was blocked well before sunset by the blizzard.

Dozing on and off, he finally pulled his legs up and wrapped his arms around them. Sitting under his makeshift shelter, he slept. The snow and wind continued to shape the landscape throughout the night, leaving the ground clear in some areas and leaving giant drifts in others.

* * *

Bart awoke, aching from immobility. There was a great pressure holding him. He opened his eyes and dim light came through the blanket over his head. He tried to move his arms, they were trapped. He pushed out with his hands. He strained pushing back with his head. He heard the snow crunch as the drift behind him collapsed.

Darkness surrounded him. Panic began to rise in him. He was buried alive under the snow! There could be several feet over him. He would quickly be out of air. He was unable to move, wrapped in a cocoon of blankets and the tarp.

Straining and struggling in his tomb of snow, he was able to gain movement of his head, shoulders, and one arm. Exhausted and gasping from the effort, he stopped. He knew that he had to keep trying because once compacted, the snow would become as hard as ice. He still had not found an opening from under the tarp.

Again, he began to twist and shove at the walls of his snowy grave. Bart fought his emotions as much as he did the snow that trapped him. He was unable to move his legs at all. They were no longer against his chest. He wiggled his toes. Knowing his legs and feet were not frozen gave him little comfort.

After what felt like an eternity, he had managed to expand the opening around his head and shoulders to little more than a foot. He pulled air deep into his lungs, trying to catch his breath. He lay in the inky blackness, trying to regain his strength.

Unexpectedly, he found himself screaming for help. His own voice was deafening in the tiny void.

Again laying still, he battled to regain control. Feeling around the small space he'd created, Bart searched for the edge of the tarp. The pounding of his heart was frightfully loud in his ears. He knew that if he didn't make headway soon, uncontrollable panic would consume him, followed by the lack of air. The end would not be far away.

Trying with every fiber of his being, Bart forced himself to stay calm. Finally, he found the edge. Forcing his fingers through the opening, he felt the sting of snow crystals. So far, his efforts had allowed him some movement from the waist up. He dug at the frozen wall with his aching fingers, bits and pieces of the compressed snow hitting his face as he burrowed upward.

All of a sudden, his hand broke through to the surface. Daylight and cold air came through the small opening. He was unable to withdraw his arm fully due to the snow that had filled part of the space created by his efforts. He breathed deeply of the fresh air. He now knew that he would not suffocate. He was also painfully aware that he could not move enough, due to the tarp and blanket around him, to gain his freedom.

Bart closed his eyes and again struggled to calm himself. He tried to move his other arm. He was unable to and panic washed over him. A hopeless wail he could not stifle came out and then became screams for help. He was losing control. He felt warmth in his lower body, which could only mean he had urinated during the effort.

Lying still and fighting for control, abruptly the light disappeared from the opening. "No!" he shouted and thrust his arm upward. His fingers grasped something. It was a . . . a rope. He felt a jerk on it.

Could it be the lead rope on one of the horses?

Hope like he had never felt before washed over him. Bart yelled, "Back! Back! Pull me up!" He continued to shout, cussing, begging, and ordering the horse to pull.

As the horse tried to get away from whatever held it, Bart felt the rope slide in his grip. He felt the snow give just a bit. If the line slipped out of his hand, he would be finished. He felt it slacken in his hand as the animal stepped closer, sniffing the familiar scent of the hand sticking out of the snow.

Bart wrapped the slack rope around his rapidly stiffening hand. Again, he shouted at the horse to pull. Startled, the animal jerked back. The lead rope cut into his hand. A cloud of desperation swept over the man and he convulsed involuntarily, shouting and screaming.

His upper body suddenly moved upward, sending unbearable pain through his immobile lower body. The crusty chunks of snow burst outward and the grip on the rope was lost. The brightness around him was blinding. The frigid air burned his throat and lungs as he gasped.

Now in the sitting position, he rested. The hand on his extended arm was blood-covered, but numb. He had to squint to see it in the bright whiteness. Beyond his arm he could see the buckskin. He tried to calm it, but his words were hoarse, unrecognizable sounds.

Bart found that his other arm was able to move. He pushed large chunks of crusty snow away from himself. Soon, he was clear to the waist. Being pulled by the buckskin had allowed some movement around his legs. After kicking and twisting his legs around, he created enough space to work his way out of the snowy grave.

Sitting, too weak to stand, he stared at the hole he had just gotten out of. The brightness around him forced him to continue to squint. Bart put his hands inside his coat, trying to warm them enough to grip the items left in the hole. His choppers were still in there and he had to get them.

The buckskin came up from behind and nudged him with its nose. He reached back and took hold of the bridle. He slowly pulled himself to his feet. Standing on wobbly legs, Bart pushed it away from the hole.

He realized how lucky he was that the horse hadn't stepped over the edge of the slope. It would have broken through and the flailing hooves may have finished him. Working his way to the remaining packs on the horse, he dug into them and brought out a pair of woolen socks.

He was beginning to shiver. He had not been able to close the loops on the coat. He clumsily worked at getting the socks over his hands. Using his teeth and the almost useless hands, he got them covered. He then hugged the horse's neck, attempting to gain some warmth.

Finally, his legs stopped shaking and he was able to stand. Looking over the back of the buckskin, he saw the paint pawing the snow-covered ground, looking for something to eat. Having not lost his livestock was an enormous relief. He looked into the distance and saw the grove of trees that had been just a shadow the day before.

Managing to get his coat loops over the bone buttons, Bart prevented the cold air from chilling him.

Getting down, he sat at the corner of the hole he had just crawled out of. He pulled out one of the blankets. One of his leather choppers came with it. He then lay across the opening and reached down, searching for the other.

He felt the corner of the other Hudson Bay blankets, the one that had covered his legs. Pulling and jerking at the blanket, he finally pulled it free. He next found the other glove. Sitting, he removed the socks from his hand. He shuddered when he saw the torn palm on his hand and how his finger nails had been severely ripped back.

When the hand regained full feeling, he would suffer from the pain. With the choppers in place, he stood in the hole and broke chunks of snow away. He pulled out the canteen, which was frozen solid. Then, crawling out, he pulled at the tarp. It was frozen to the ground and much of it was still tight under the snow.

Giving up on saving the tarp, he gathered the two blankets and canteen. These he managed to tie on the back of the buckskin. Leading the horse, he walked, stumbling as he broke through the snow crust. The paint reached out its nose as he approached, looking for a treat from its master.

Bart decided to head directly to the trees and build a fire to warm up and dry his clothing. His breeches were frozen stiff in the mid-section from being wet during one of his moments of panic. He loosened the cinch on the paint and decided to try and walk the short distance to the trees.

By the time he got there, he was again sweating. Quickly, he put together some twigs and bark, along with some tufts of grass. Striking the flint over the tinder, he soon had a fire going. There was an abundance of dead wood and he build a large fire. He put the canteen near enough to melt its contents.

Rigging some branches, he made a drying rack for his clothing. The bright sun on the snow made his face hurt from squinting. The heat from his fire made him painfully aware of all the other scrapes and cuts he had suffered. His back also ached from being wrenched when pulled loose from the snowy tomb by the buckskin.

He stood in his boots and woolen long johns while his clothing dried. Meanwhile, he put snow into his pots to melt. As soon at the water began to boil, he would make coffee and start a hot soup. Sitting on a log he had dragged over, Bart sipped warm water while waiting for the coffee to be ready. His throat was raw from screaming while buried.

His lungs remained sore from breathing in the frosty air. Pouring a cup of coffee, he allowed it to cool for a moment while he added beans and pork to the pot. He then dropped in two small now frozen onions he had gotten from the trading post. After adding some salt to the pot, he sat back to drink the coffee.

The wind continued to blow across the open plains, carrying wisps of snow. He had to keep turning near the fire to keep all sides warm. By the time the soup was done, he had been able to get dressed. The breeches took the longest to dry, due to additional cleaning.

After a full day of not eating any food, and even longer since he'd had something hot, the soup was very satisfying. Bart continued adding wood to the fire as he slowly worked his way through the pot of soup. Now he felt warm, inside and out.

Nearby the horses dug through the snow for

brown grass, or chew on tender ends of the better tasting bushes. No longer hungry, Bart got out the brush and groomed both horses. The effort helped keep him warm. He found some sores on the paint from wearing the saddle through the storm. Until they healed, he would ride the buckskin.

Moving them to some grazing closer to his fire, he sat having the last cup of coffee and watching the sun set as it sent a blaze of red across the western sky. He had made up his bed in front of a pile of brush. It would reflect the heat of the fire and keep the wind off him. That night he slept poorly, having nightmares of being trapped.

Waking just after sunrise, Bart's body ached from his ordeal. He had a deep, wracking cough. His eyes were red and burning from the brightness of the snow the day before. There were high clouds that morning, which would help to cut the glare.

With coffee water on, he sliced strips of side meat into his frying pan. He then mixed some sourdough bread and set it aside to fry in the grease after the meat was done. As he turned to look at the horses, pain shot through his back and he moaned. He would have to be careful how he moved.

Turning slowly back, he stared at his hand that had held the lead rope. It ached from being sprained as well as cut. After eating, he would clean the torn skin and bandage it. The leather chopper would protect it from further damage. It was his left hand, and thankfully he wore the revolver on his right.

The sun was high in the morning sky when he moved out toward the river. Under his coat was a package of fried bread and bacon to be eaten later. The horses broke through the crust as they walked. Bart tried to keep the animals to the clean ground whenever possible.

With luck, he would be at the South Platte River by late tomorrow. He would soon see Pike's Peak in the distance. He had been in the area more than once and the landmarks would be familiar.

CHAPTER SEVENTEEN

Ten years before, Bart had guided some hunters and they had resupplied at Fort Jackson on the Platte. The following year, it had been closed. The owner had completely destroyed the trading post before leaving.

He had heard that another man had opened a trading post a day's ride into the mountains from the site of Fort Jackson. Most trading posts had a difficult time staying in business since the beaver pelt market had disappeared. Men's hats were now made with silk rather than beaver.

Bart rode looking at the snow-covered top of Pike's Peak. The exposed granite had a reddish color. The sun was beginning to melt the snow of the early winter storm. Bart removed his coat and tied it to the back of the saddle. While it would be comfortable throughout the day, the nights on the high desert plains would be frigid.

Taking a deep breath of the air reminded him of spring. He began to cough again. Bart hoped the icy air he had breathed during the storm wouldn't cause the cough to develop into something worse.

Patting the horse's neck, he laughed. "Considering the bastard I'm looking for, I am in pretty damn bad shape. A half-healed rib, sore back, aching hand, and a cough that makes breathing deep impossible. The son-of-a-bitch will only have to give me an angry stare and I will be done."

Bart reached the South Platte River in the early afternoon. Swinging down from the buckskin, he let the horses drink. He dumped the water from his canteen and refilled it with the cold water.

His plan was to follow the river north until he found the ruins of Fort Jackson. From there he would follow the streams and rivers into the mountains, looking for a cabin or evidence of someone trapping. He doubted being able to find Bruno before spring. He hoped that the man he hunted had resupplied at the trading post.

Deciding to spend the night, Bart pulled out some line and a fish hook. Soon, he was set to try and catch supper. Sitting next to the slowly moving river, he thought back to his youth. He and his brother had often talked of fishing and hunting in the west once they were older.

Using pieces of the fried bread as bait, it did not take long before he had several nice bluegills lying on the bank. By the time he had a cook fire going, the chill of the evening forced him to drape a blanket over his shoulders. Squatting next to the fire, he fried fish for his supper. He enjoyed the change of fare. He saved another six fish for his breakfast.

Sitting next to the fire, huddled under his blanket, he sipped on the last of his evening coffee. It was getting to be late December. He didn't know the date exactly and it might even be Christmas. He realized that due to drinking, he remembered little of the past several Christmases.

If it weren't for the men he had been hunting, he and Millie would be celebrating their first holiday together. The ache of missing her was with him every day. The anger he felt for those he hunted could be pushed to the back of his mind, only to return with full heat when something triggered a memory of their actions.

Bart crawled into his blankets and stared up at the stars. It was a moonless night, and the points of light in the heavens looked larger than normal. He worried that physically he was not up to the coming fight. Even something as simple as a coughing spell could render him helpless at the wrong time.

He could shoot Bruno Pascal from a distance when he found him. The man would be dead, but Bart's need to face and hurt the man had to be satisfied. He wanted to see the man's face up close, when Pascal realized he was going to die. He wanted the man to know that it was because of what he had done to Millie that he was to lose his life.

He laid for hours, unable to stop thinking. Hatred was a terrible and dangerous thing. It could cause a man to go carelessly into harm's way. Many a man had died trying to right a wrong due to blind anger.

Morning came and Bart had slept little. He felt sick inside. Sick because Pascal had not only caused the death of someone he loved, but could quite possibly rob him of his sanity. Bart had known a settler who'd had his family killed by the Cherokee. The man had attempted to find and kill those who'd hurt him. He was eventually found running, hatless and shoeless, on the prairie, attacking shadows with a stick.

Bart made a quick breakfast out of the

remaining fish. The pleasure he had felt the night before was gone. He ate quickly and then got his gear together. He felt driven to hurry and find Bruno.

Snow began to fall shortly after he started riding. The wind was blowing gently and the immediate threat of another blizzard was slim. It took two hours to reach the fort ruins. The South Platte River wound in and out of the plain. He had followed it north. In some cases, he had ridden in the water to pass through sections that had granite walls rising on both sides.

Bart passed the Vasquez River, which flowed into the South Platte River. It had been named after Louis Vasquez, who had trapped in the area. The next creek flowing into the Platte was Boulder Creek. It flowed from a valley leading into the foothills of the Rocky Mountains. This was the creek where the new trading post was located.

It was nearly sunset and still snowing when he saw the low log building. A buckskin-clad man with a full beard was chopping wood for the evening fire. Bart stopped the buckskin short of the trading post. For a moment, he thought that the man he was looking at could have been Pascal. He then realized that the man was tall and thickly built.

Urging the horse forward, he hailed the cabin. The wood chopper set the axe down and watched him ride in. Stopping short of the man, Bart swung down. "The name is Bart Nevell."

The tall mountain man wiped his hand on the side of his leather shirt. "Pleased to meet you, Bart. I'm Tom, Tom Franklin."

The man stepped forward to shake Bart's hand. "My wife just finished making a nice bear stew. Put your horses in the stable. You'll find it just beyond the trading post. I'll get this wood hauled in."

The heavy flakes had coated both of the horses. Leading them into the stable, he left the door open to allow a little light in. Bart then brushed the snow off the animals and stripped the gear. After putting them into empty stalls, he grabbed a pitch fork and tossed some hay to the horses.

Putting the saddle on the edge of the buckskin's stall, he picked up his saddlebags and the bundle with his blankets. Heading across the barnyard, he noticed a soft light coming from the trading post windows. It would be dark in less than a half-hour.

Kicking the snow off his boots, Bart pulled the latch string on the door and stepped into the large warm room. Tom's wife was just doing the final touches to a long table located at the back of the room. Looking around, Bart saw that there were shelves on both sides, filled with goods for sale.

Wolf, bear, and beaver traps hung from pegs driven into the logs. Rolls of leather and coils of rope sat on the floor below the traps. The shelves were stocked with canned goods, bags of flour and coffee, kerosene cans and lamps, blankets similar to the ones Bart purchased, and bolts of cloth. A shelf near the door had a row of corked jugs. They were probably filled with rye.

The room was a blend of smells of the rope and leather. He also smelled baked bread and the stew. Tom was stacking the wood near a large stone fireplace. In the middle of the room was a ten-plate stove used for cooking as well as heat. Next to the fireplace was a sideboard used to prepare food and clean up afterward. Above it were shelves with dishes and tins containing cooking items. Dried herbs hung tied in bunches.

Bart noticed that Tom's wife was an Indian. She turned, seeing him looking around. "We have most things a trapper or hunter might need. We hope to add things settlers could use," she said, smiling. "My name is Eva." Seeing the surprise in his eyes, she added, "I am an Arapahoe. Tom and I were married after he saved me from Comancheros."

"Excuse me staring," Bart said, blushing. "You are a beautiful woman, but I was having trouble placing the tribe."

Just then, an old, white-haired Indian came from the back, leading a small boy. "I smelled the stew and hoped it was time to eat." Seeing Bart standing awkwardly in the middle of the room, he nodded. "I am Two Buffalo, a famous Cheyenne chief."

Tom finished piling the wood and came to the aid of the visitor. "Give the man some space to breathe. It appears you have met everyone, Bart. Except for the young one, he is Isaac."

Shortly, they were seated at the table with plates filled with the tasty stew and slices of fresh bread. They drank coffee with chicory. There was honey on the table to sweeten the drink, or spread on the bread.

Young Isaac sat on his mother's lap and helped himself to bread with honey from her plate. Two Buffalo told stories of the past, his creased face breaking into a smile as he told of once saving Tom from a cougar.

Bart watched the friendly conversation between the family members. He felt the warmth at the table. He'd had this with Millie for the short time after she came to the ranch. After eating, they sat again at the table with fresh coffee. Eva went and got a plate out from behind a curtained shelf.

Young Isaac squealed with joy. In her hand was a plate of cookies. "I was saving these for Christmas day, but I think they will go well with our guest tonight."

She set the plate in front of Bart, taking one to give to the excited child. Looking at the cookies, Bart wondered why the Franklins were so quick to take in a stranger. Maybe it was because of the holiday. It could be the news he would bring from the outside world.

Bart took a cookie and passed the plate to Tom. "I am not sure what day it is. When is Christmas?" he asked.

"It is two days away," Tom said. "Eva will be busy putting up a tree tomorrow. We have a ham hanging out back for Christmas dinner."

"I best look in on the stock," Tom said.

Getting up quickly, Bart agreed. "I need to rub some liniment on the paint. It had the saddle on during the blizzard and developed some sore spots."

Following Tom out into the cold, Bart began to cough when the frosty air hit his lungs. Stopping to catch his breath, he stood with his hands on his knees. Tom came back to make sure he was alright.

"That is a hell of a cough, my friend," Tom said.

Concentrating on taking shallow breaths, he replied, almost in a whisper, "Took in some cold air and damaged my lungs a little during the storm."

"When we get back in, I'll have Eva put some balsam and a few other things in a pot and let you breathe the vapors. It works for me every time."

While he took care of the horses, Bart watched Tom pitching hay to the animals. "Two Buffalo mentioned being a famous chief. I didn't recognize the name."

"I think he is more famous in our eyes than the Cheyenne," Tom said.

That night, Bart made up his bed in front of the fireplace. The concoction that Eva put together made his breathing much more comfortable. She saved it to heat again in the morning. When he said that he would be leaving the next morning, they insisted he stay until after Christmas. No one should be alone on such a day.

Lying in his blankets, Bart was happy that they had talked him into staying. He needed the time to mend, and the trading post was a warm and happy place. Tomorrow, he would ask Tom about the trapper he was hunting.

It was still dark when Bart awoke. It was not because of any discomfort, but rather an excitement of the holiday coming. As a youngster, his father would drink too much holiday cheer, and it had almost always caused violent behavior. His mother would often hide him and his brother to shield them from their father's temper.

Bart got the fire going in the stove. Breaking the ice on top of the water bucket, he filled the coffee pot and put it on the stove to heat. He noticed that more fire wood needed to be brought in. Slipping his heavy coat on, he stepped outside. The crisp air froze the hair in his nose. Breathing vapors of Eva's mixture had done some good. He was able to control the cough.

Walking to the woodpile, he heard the snow

crunching under his boots. Bart had grown up in the south and had seen little snow until he'd joined the army. It was exciting to see at first. As the winter dragged on, it was less pleasurable.

Testing the edge of the axe with his thumb, Bart found it to properly sharpened. Pulling his choppers out from under his coat, he pulled them on and started working on the wood. It was not long until his coat lay on the ground next to him and a large pile of split wood lay on the other side.

It felt good to swing the axe. He had done hard work in his life and had always been naturally strong. Kneeling, Bart piled a large armload of wood, using his knee to support the arm while he stacked it. Grunting as he stood up, he walked back to the trading post. He was dumping the wood near the fireplace when Tom came from the bedroom.

"I'll help you with the wood. Eva will need a lot to cook everything for tomorrow's meal." He and Bart brought in several armloads. With the task complete, they added grounds to the coffee pot and were soon drinking the morning brew.

Eva got up and stood next to the stove, warming up. "In one moment I will warm the mixture for your cough."

After some more coffee and a treatment for his lungs, Bart went to put his coat on. "I will water and feed the stock."

"Not alone," Tom said.

"I'll have breakfast ready when you get back," Eva promised.

Walking to the stable, Bart noticed a small building next to the creek. It had a large chimney for such a small structure.

Seeing him looking at the building, Tom said, "It's a sauna."

"A sauna?" Bart asked.

"I met a Finnish fellow while coming west from Albany. He talked of taking steam baths back in Finland. Told me how they built the sauna. When we settled here I put this one up." Laughing, Tom continued, "I can only imagine what Oli would think if he saw this here in the mountains."

"I know a man named Oli. He's a good man. Mr. August taught me a lot about backing up a friend," Bart said, thinking about the blond man.

"Oli August?" Tom said, astonished at hearing the name. "I think we are talking about the same man."

"Isaac, Oli talked of a boy named Isaac that was killed and buried near the Ohio River. I should have known, you named your son after your brother."

Tom smiled, "Yes, we did. He and I were to become trappers together." After reflecting a moment, he said, "I am glad to hear Oli is well. He had something he had to do in the west."

For an hour they talked of Oli, while watering and feeding the stock. On the way back to the trading post, Tom told Bart that they would be warming the sauna today.

The sauna was a two-room building. One was for drying off and dressing, the other for taking steam and washing. The wash room had a three-level bench. A stone fireplace with tin tub for heating water stood in one corner. They would throw water on the rocks to make steam.

Bart looked over his cuts and bruises as he sat on the upper bench. His back was better, his rib had quit hurting, his cough was gone. The steam was great for his bruised body.

* * *

Christmas was a day of food, gifts, songs, and prayer. An evergreen tree was set up in the main room. It was decorated with popcorn strings and paper snowflakes. Isaac ran around the room chasing Two Buffalo with a small bow the old chief had given him. Gifts were simple, and handmade. Bart had nothing to share but was assured that being with friends was what was important.

After the meal, they sat resting. Eva went into a back room and brought out a deerskin coat. She placed it in front of Bart. "Tom and I want you to have this. It will keep you warm and dry. I made it for Tom. It was too big, so I made a second one for him."

Embarrassed, Bart looked at the well-crafted coat. "I can't take this. Besides I have a coat."

"Two Buffalo likes your coat. You give it to him and keep this for yourself," Tom suggested.

Before he went to sleep that night, he had a fine deerskin coat and the chief was sitting proudly in the Hudson Bay blanket coat.

CHAPTER EIGHTEEN

The morning after Christmas, Bart was helping Tom clean the stable. Tom was talking about trying to get a couple of milk cows and a bull. He had grown up in Vermont, where they had made cheese and butter on the family farm.

Bart had purposely not asked about the trapper he was looking for. The joy he had experienced would go a long way in healing his injured soul. He didn't want to bring anything up that might create a cloud over the holiday.

Now it was time to continue the search. He asked Tom, "I have been looking for a trapper, he's got one eye. The man may be traveling with a Ute woman. He hasn't stopped in the trading post, has he?"

Tom pitched a fork full of soiled bedding out the hatch in the wall. Frowning, he turned to Bart. "I met him. He came in here looking for traps. Treated the woman kinda rough." Tossing another forkful out, he asked, "You got dealings with him?"

"He owes me for something in Waco," Bart replied.

With a questioning look on his face, Tom said, "He talked of heading for the Vasquez River. There's an old miner, named Toby, has a cabin on the river.

He might know more."

Not wanting to end the feeling of harmony he had found at the trading post, Bart decided to stay one more night before leaving. If Bruno had settled on the river for the winter, an extra day wouldn't matter.

Bart made another decision. He was going to leave the paint with Tom. Pascal would recognize the horse as Smoke's. If things worked out on the Vasquez River, he would come back and get it. If not, he couldn't think of a better place for the horse.

Tom agreed to keep the paint for Bart. He again warned him about what type of man he was going to find. Thanking him for his concern, the big man saddled the buckskin and loaded his gear.

Riding down Boulder Creek, he then went south on the Platte. By early afternoon he was at the fork of the Vasquez. The buckskin was pushing through knee-deep snow. The horse had the legs to handle snow.

After resting at the fork, Bart and his horse moved slowly toward the mountains, following the Vasquez River. The white world of snow was in stark contrast to the dark form of the rider. The wind coming from the northwest filled the tracks with blowing snow, leaving only a scant depression in the frozen plain to show their passing.

Tilting his head to cut the wind, Bart was pleased with the deerskin coat. It kept him warm and blowing snow didn't stick to it. He didn't know how far up the river the miner's cabin was located. He could see a stand of pine trees in the valley ahead of him. He would reach it within the hour and planned to spend the night.

It began to snow right after Bart had set up

camp. He chose an evergreen with branches low to the ground. Clearing the dead branches from one side of the trunk, he made a small fire and put water on to heat. He picketed Buck on a patch of grass blown clear of snow. Later, he would move the horse under the pines for protection from the weather.

Eva had sent him off with bread and thick slices of ham. Bart set the frying pan next to the flames and put the ham to warm. He fashioned some sticks to hold slices of bread. Once the ham was warm, he would toast the bread. When the water was boiling, he added a mixture of coffee and chicory, giving it a stir to stop the foaming.

With the meal eaten and the horse safely under the trees, Bart made up his bed under some protective branches. The weather had cleared and the wind was still. Curled up in his blankets with only the glow of the coals of his fire for light, he was warm and relaxed. He didn't know what hardships and dangers would be encountered in the next few days, but tonight he thought about the past days and Christmas with the Franklins.

* * *

The threat of snow in the gray sky and a north wind greeted Bart the next morning. Clumps of snow falling from the branches made starting his morning fire a challenge. He finally had coffee brewed. He warmed the last of the bread near the fire. Dunking the bread in his mug of coffee, he chewed slowly and stared up the river.

Before saddling the horse, he checked his weapons. He fired the Colt Dragoon first. After cleaning and reloading it, he did the same with his Hawken rifle. With his razor-sharp knife in his boot, Bart felt ready to face whatever came his way.

Biting pellets of snow stung his face as he rode the buckskin beside the river. Along with watching the valley ahead of him, Bart kept his eye on the storm developing around him. He didn't want to be caught a second time.

The horse had to bust through several chest-high drifts. Once, it stumbled into a snow-covered brook and almost threw the man over its head. At one point Bart walked, leading the animal to give it some relief. He pushed through snow as deep as his waist, stopping frequently to catch his breath.

Bart smelled the wood smoke before he came upon the cabin. It looked like a large snow drift with a tunnel dug to the front door. A column of smoke hung heavy above the cabin. Once above the pine trees surrounding the cabin, it was whisked away by the wind. The Vasquez River ran nearby

He tied the buckskin under some pines a short distance from the cabin. He started to pull the rifle and changed his mind. Patting the horse on its shoulder, he pulled the choppers up on his hands and headed toward the door. The plank door had the latchstring pulled in. He pounded on the door.

The sound of the latch being lifted let Bart know the occupant was inside. The door swung open. An Indian woman stepped back into the shadows. He followed her into the dimly lit room. A sooty lantern sat on a wooden table. A man stood in front of the fireplace and was adding a chunk of wood.

"Welcome stranger," the man said, turning to face Bart.

Bart froze briefly as he saw the patch over one eye. He realized that the Dragoon was under his coat and he still had the choppers on his hands. Forcing himself to act casually, he forced a smile.

"Thanks, it feels good to get out of that damn snow," he replied. "Came here looking for a hot meal from Toby. Thought this was his cabin."

"He's out digging for gold. The Ute and I are wintering with him. Shuck your coat, give it to the woman," Bruno said.

Hoping that Pascal thought he was a friend just passing through, Bart needed to improve his fighting position. Pulling off his choppers, he then slipped off the heavy deerskin coat.

The Ute took it and he turned back to face the one-eyed man. He felt a tug at his side and put his hand down. His gun was gone. The woman had taken it as soon as he had turned away.

"What the hell's going on here? Why'd she take the gun?" Bart demanded.

"We can't be too careful. You might be here to steal Toby's gold."

Bart knew that the miner wasn't away digging for gold. The latchstring would have been hanging outside for him to use when he returned. If the miner Toby had lived here, he no longer did.

Bruno stood in front of him with only a knife on his hip. His rifle was elsewhere in the cabin. The woman behind Bart had not cocked the heavy Colt Dragoon. Anger was surging through the big man's body as he faced the man that had hurt Millie.

All of a sudden, the expression on Bruno's face changed. There was an excitement of recognition. "Ain't you someone I saw in Waco? You didn't have a beard then, but a man your size ain't likely to be forgotten."

Feeling confident with the knife in his boot, Bart decided to confront Pascal. "The name's Bart Nevell. Millie and I lived together on the ranch."

"Millie? Hell, you mean the gal we played with down in Texas." Bruno's eye was shining as he looked at Bart. He settled his hand on the butt of his knife. "She were fun, cowboy. Just enough fight to make it sport. The Ute over there got no spunk at all. I may go back to Waco and have another go at her, come spring."

Bart fought to control his emotions. He knew Pascal was taunting him to make him reckless. He already had the big man dead and buried in his mind. "Where is the miner?" he asked Bruno.

"He up and died, poor old man. I believe he bled to death. He didn't want to share his gold. It took a while to convince him that he had more than he needed," Bruno laughed. He had drawn his knife. "You should have passed him in his watery grave when you rode up the river."

Bart pulled the knife from his boot. The table was between them. The big man began to move around the table to the side of Pascal's blind eye.

"When I get done cutting on you, you'll be crying just like your woman did. Maybe I'll let my Ute have her way with you before we end your misery. She does things with fire that you won't believe."

Bart glanced at the floor to make sure there was nothing to trip over. Noticing this, Bruno made his move. He shoved the table at the big man and followed close behind, thrusting the knife low. Turning sideways, the deadly knife narrowly missed his midsection as the trapper swept by. Before Bart could regain his footing, the man was by him and poised for his next attack.

The wiry trapper was fast and knew how to fight with a knife. Nevell had always depended on his strength to win a close contact fight. His friend Oli could hit an ant with a knife at 10 paces. Bart had thrown a knife before, but had no confidence in doing so.

He continued to circle with the trapper. Twice, Pascal drew blood with a quick move and slash. The cut left on Bart's cheek had blood running down his neck. Another on his free arm stung as the woolen shirt rubbed against it.

The Ute woman sat in the corner with the Dragoon in her lap. She stared wide-eyed at the two men fighting. The heavy clothing was slowing the big man down more than usual. Sweat was running down his back.

He stepped back, trying to get closer to the woman with his gun. "You try and grab your gun. She will shoot you right in the belly," Bruno threatened.

Bart noticed that his coat was within reach. He waited as the trapper moved back and forth in front of him. Pascal was now playing with the big man. He planned to continue making slashing cuts until his quarry collapsed from exhaustion or loss of blood. Bart, acting tired, lowered his arms a bit.

Smiling, Bruno stepped forward to inflict the next cut. Bart grabbed the heavy deerskin coat and threw it at Bruno. It engulfed the man's arms. Stepping in, the big man knocked the blade aside under the coat and wrapped his arms around the trapper, pinning the knife hand between their bodies.

Locking his arms around the wiry waist, Bart squeezed the man's back with all his strength. If Bruno was able to twist free, he would thrust his knife into the big man's stomach, ending the fight.

Like a wild cat, Pascal twisted and squirmed, he bit at Bart's face and neck. He tried to head butt the nose, but the big man had his head turned. He kicked and tried to knee the groin.

Bart could hear screaming in his ears. It was his own voice as he raged. Holding Bruno in a death grip, the big man heaved his chest and pulled into the smaller man's back. He felt the spine give and Bruno cry out. The small man went limp.

Dragging him over to the cot in the corner, not daring to release his grip for fear the man might be playing possum, he tossed him onto the bed and grabbed the coat, pulling if off the small man. He heard the knife fall to the floor.

Pascal lay still, his face frozen in pain. Picking the fallen knife up, Bart staggered back and leaned against the table, struggling to catch his breath. At any moment he expected to be shot by the woman, and he was too weak to resist.

He heard a step as she came toward him. Looking over, he saw her handing him the gun. She took Pascal's knife from his hand and headed out the door. Looking down at the gun, he noticed blood running out from under his shirt cuff and down the back of his hand.

Bruno was groaning on the bunk. Bart saw the man freeze with pain every time he tried to move. The door opened and the woman came back in. She had a piece of bark covered with pine pitch. She motioned him to sit on a chair.

She placed the bark on the table and helped him remove his shirt. She pointed at two additional spots the knife had cut. She smeared the pine pitch on each of the cuts and then covered them with cobwebs from the cabin rafters. The sticky covering stopped the bleeding and held the cuts closed.

The cut on his arm was the deepest, so she also wrapped it with a strip of cloth. Bart had regained his wind and was beginning to feel a chill. Moving over to the fire place, he put his shirt back on. The woman put a pot of water next to the crackling fire and began to put a meal together.

Physically and emotionally exhausted, he accepted the beans with venison she offered. She made some type of tea for him to drink. They sat gazing at the suffering Bruno. He now lay staring at them with his good eye, his mouth hanging open. Drool was running down the side of his jaw.

With the meal finished and the sweat in his clothing dried, Bart was ready to leave. He thought about shooting the heartless man before he went, but decided leaving him paralyzed was a more fitting punishment.

With his knife and revolver back in their places, he picked up the heavy deerskin coat. He looked at the man lying in the cot. "You best treat this woman well. You have to depend on her to help keep you alive from now on."

"Don't leave me with her. Kill me, you damn coward. Finish what you started and kill me," Bruno hissed.

Ignoring the man's plea, Bart said, "I am taking the horse you stole and bringing it back to the owner."

Bart turned to leave after thanking the woman.

He could hear the broken man calling after him to come back. Locating the stolen horse, he led it out of the stable. As he walked toward the buckskin, Bart could hear Pascal shouting threats at the Ute woman. Climbing into the saddle, he rode from the cabin, leading the extra horse.

Hardly noticed along the stream was the unspoiled beauty of the snow-covered ground and trees. As he rode away, there came the sound of Bruno crying, "No, no . . ." followed by prolonged screaming. Bart ignored the pleas. The big man had only one thought in mind: There was still another man out there who he had to find. Millie had said that there had been four.

CHAPTER NINETEEN

There were only a couple of hours of sunlight left. Bart continued to hear Bruno screaming and cussing as he worked his way from the cabin. He kept the buckskin in the same tracks from their arrival, making going a little easier. Arriving at the stand of pine where he had spent the night, he dismounted and led the two horses under cover.

He could make Pueblo in three days of hard riding. That is, if another storm didn't make travel impossible. Snow had blown in under the tree. Shoving it with his feet, he cleared an area to camp. After finding some grass for the horses to graze, he got the fire going and made some coffee.

The big man felt numb inside. To the best of his knowledge, he had taken care of the worst of the four men. The trapper had probably caused the damage that had killed Millie. He had expected to feel relief, but none came.

He wondered what the miner had been like. Bruno had killed Toby to find his gold. The hard-earned dust and nuggets were no doubt hidden in the cabin. He wished that he had caught up to Pascal sooner and saved the old man.

After a meal of jerky and coffee, he brought the

horses in under the pines and spread out his bedroll. Lying awake, he stared into the night. A few stars peeked in through the branches. The howls of wolves were a lonely sound. The night would be cold.

An hour after he fell asleep, the sound of an animal moving beyond his camp woke him. Bart lay listening, holding his breath to hear. It was coming toward his camp. Maybe it was an elk using their trail for walking. He glanced at the coals of his fire.

The sound stopped and he heard a snort. There was the creaking of a saddle as someone dismounted. Bart withdrew his Colt Dragoon from under his saddle. He wished that he had thrown snow over the coals. There was the crunching of footsteps coming toward the tree.

"You'd best stop where you are, or I'll cut loose with this Colt," he warned.

A voice came back, speaking a Plains Indian tongue that he recognized. "It is me, the woman from the cabin."

Replying in the same language, Bart said, "Stay where you are. I'll come out."

Pulling his boots on, he put on the coat that he had been using for a top cover. Ducking under the branches, the big man stared at his visitor. She stood next to the trapper's horse. The moon was just coming up, its soft light glistening on the snow.

"Let me take care of the horse. Put some wood on the fire," he told her.

Leading the horse to the others, he tied it to a thick branch and stripped the saddle. He felt something cold and wet hanging from the saddle horn. When he got back to the fire, he could see that it was a scalp.

Looking at the Ute woman, he said, "I see you took his hair. He might get cold without it."

Without a smile, she said, "His back no longer bothers him and he is very warm."

Looking around the small area under the tree, Bart pushed more snow away for her to make up a bed. "You can sleep there," he said.

Pulling his boots off, he crawled back under his blankets and spread the heavy coat on top. The woman went away briefly. When she came back, she picked up the edge of his blanket. "The night is cold, I will keep you warm," she said.

The next morning, Bart took care of the horses while the woman made them something to eat. After a quick breakfast, he readied the horses for travel. He put his saddle on the Mexican's mustang to give the buckskin a rest. He watched as the woman walked to the edge of the river.

Opening the top of a leather bag, she began to spread the contents into the Vasquez River. It shined like gold as it splashed into the water. Looking inside, she tied the bag to her waist.

She saw Bart staring at her. "It is the old man's gold. I put it back in the river with him to quiet his spirit."

* * *

There were only a few inches of snow in Pueblo. He bid the woman goodbye as she headed for her village. The trapper's horse would give her something to use when returning to her people. That morning, she had checked his knife wounds and nodded with satisfaction at the way they were healing.

He was leading the mustang and headed straight for the Mexican's house. Swinging down in front of the adobe building, he tied the buckskin to a post. Turning, he heard the door open. It was the Mexican, with a blanket wrapped around his shoulders.

"You have brought back my horse, señor," he said, smiling broadly.

"Yes I have, Mario," Bart replied. "I need you to do something for me in the spring."

"Anything, señor, you just ask and I will do it," the Mexican said, taking the lead rope.

"I am going to buy two milk cows and a bull. I need to have them taken to a trading post, a day's ride up the Boulder Creek from the South Platte River. "

"It will be done. I will do this for you, señor," the man proudly affirmed. Suddenly, he noticed the pitch-covered cut on the big man's face. "The man that cut me also cut you. I am sorry. I did not mean for you to risk your life for the horse."

"Trust me amigo, it wasn't because of the horse," Bart said, then he paused a moment. "The man that cut you . . . he is no more."

"He was a man that deserved to die."

"One more thing," Bart added. "The trading post is owned by a man named Tom Franklin. He has a horse, a paint that I left with him. For your trouble, you can have it."

"No, No, señor," Mario protested, "bringing back my mustang is enough."

Continuing, he said, "I insist. I will write a note giving you ownership."

After giving the Mexican a note, he led the buckskin to the trading post. Inside, he found Peck busy stocking shelves. A long overdue shipment had just arrived.

Seeing Bart coming in the door, he stopped and went to pour some coffee for the big man. "See you got back without freezing or getting yourself killed."

Accepting the mug, Bart smiled. "It was nip and tuck on both. I managed to keep a step ahead of the reaper."

"Word is you brought the Ute woman back. I hope you killed the son-of-a-bitch that bought her."

"I put a hurting on him, but it was the woman that finished the deed," Bart said.

Savoring the coffee, he set the mug down. "Peck, I need to buy a couple milk cows and a bull. The Mexican, Mario, will drive them to a family up in the mountains come spring."

Smiling, Peck said, "That I can help you with. In the morning, I will take you to a ranch south of here that has some they'd sell."

* * *

The ride back to Texas was cold and long. It was the first week of February when Bart rode down the main street of Waco. Remnants of a recent snow were on the side of the muddy street. He was sporting a long beard and was in need of a haircut. In his buckskin coat, he looked every bit a man of the mountains.

He'd had one confrontation with some Comancheros that left two of them dead and caused a new hole in his hat. Another time, he was chased by some Apaches. After two days of a running battle, they had decided to find easier prey.

Riding past the Mustang Saloon, he slowed the buckskin. Changing his mind, he continued south to see Wolfgang.

The old friend was sweeping mud chunks from his front walk when Bart rode up. Looking up at the rugged man, he paused a moment before recognition. "Is that you, Bart, under all those whiskers?"

"It's me, alright. I need to rest a night before heading to the ranch."

Tossing the broom aside, Wolfgang smiled. "Well, you get on down from that horse and come on in. I got a nice pot of hot soup on."

Stiffly, Bart swung down. The buckskin was gaunt from the long trip. He loosened the cinch strap and tied the horse to the rail.

The soup was thick, but bland. It made little difference to the big man. He was hungry enough to eat prairie grass. It was about an hour before sundown. A young Mexican boy came to the trading post with his father and was sitting on the porch in front. Bart gave the young man a coin to brush, water and feed his horse.

With eyes shining, the boy led the buckskin to the river. Bart remained on the porch with his coffee. In the chill of the night he watched as the sun set in the west. The scattered clouds turned from bright gold to ruby red.

He thought about Millie. This was the kind of evening that they should have been cuddled up enjoying. A wave of loneliness and regret washed over him. He had wasted too many years before deciding to settle down. He wondered if he would have had a young son like the Mexican boy taking care of the horse.

He heard Wolfgang walking up behind him. "By the way, the stone cutter in Waco has the marker ready."

"Thanks, my friend. Tomorrow I will bring it to the ranch and set it on the grave."

Taking a seat beside Bart, the owner said, "Some of Axel's boys were in a couple weeks ago. They said the old man's not doing so well. They say he has lost his fire."

"Losing someone you love can do that to a man," Bart replied.

"You best watch out for him. Word is, he is waiting to face you," Wolfgang warned.

"I still have one man to find. I just hope he is willing to let me finish what I set out to do."

The next morning, the sun was just above the horizon when Bart rode towards Waco. Wolfgang filled him up with a good portion of porridge before he left. He was wearing cleaner clothes and the deerskin coat. Bart had cleaned up a bit in the back room.

Riding up to the Mustang Saloon, Bart tied the horse to the rail and walked inside. Tony was talking to some cowboys at the end of the bar. Looking up, he gave a double take. "You kind a resemble someone I know, but sure as hell don't look like him. Is that you, Bart?"

"It's me, back from the mountains. I hoped you had found out who the fourth man was."

Shaking his head, the bartender came around the end of the bar. "No, Bart, I haven't heard. Talk of what happened has kind of died down. You still drinking coffee?"

The big man sat at a table. "That would be

mighty fine."

The two men sat, catching up on things. "I saw Joshua and his boy in town last week. They were getting supplies. A couple of no-goods were giving him a hard time. I sent the bums on their way. He has a fine-looking son there."

Bart thought about them being alone on the ranch. "I worry about them a bit. Joshua has a good head on his shoulders. He should do alright."

* * *

Leading a pack horse borrowed from Junior's livery, Bart arrived at the ranch. Nate and Mary were playing outside the bunkhouse. He noticed that the ranch house remained as he had left it. Riding up to the children, he stopped. Wide-eyed, they looked up at him.

"Did you forget me already?" he teased.

With squeals of delight they ran forward, Nate taking the buckskins reins, while Mary called to their mother. Sara came out of the house shading her eyes.

"Boss Bart, you need a shave and haircut. You look like someone right off the cover of a eastern magazine," she kidded.

"Joshua around?" he asked.

Looking down, her smile disappeared. "He and Samuel is rounding the cattle up and moving them closer in."

"Was there trouble?" he asked, seeing her change of mood.

"We've been having riders go by. Some cattle have been taken, others have been shot and left to rot."

Bart's face tightened. No doubt some didn't

like having a black family running a farm on their own. It put them above their station.

Suddenly smiling again, Sara looked at Bart. "Don't you worry about us. We will make out fine. I will have Nate kill a chicken for supper after he takes care of your horse."

Quickly, she instructed the youngsters and they were off doing her bidding. Bart led the packhorse to the stand of oak trees. Millie's grave was well taken care of by Sara. Soon the flowers should start leafing out and there would be blooms by summer.

Taking the stone off the packhorse, Bart placed it at the head of the grave. Tamping the dirt down around it, he stepped back. He was so focused on his task that he didn't hear the horse come up behind him.

"Hey, Nevell. I see you're back."

Turning, he watched as Axel Gerber swung off his horse. The elderly man stared at Bart with piercing eyes. "I heard it in town."

Bart stepped away from the grave, his Dragoon under the deerskin coat. "There is still one man I have to find. Once I do that, I will come back and face you as I promised."

Axel dropped the reins and moved away from his horse. His coat was pulled back with the butt of the Paterson showing.

"There ain't any fourth man to look for."

"Before Millie died, she said there were four. I made a promise to her that I would find them and they would pay," Bart said, trying to reason with the man.

Axel shifted uncomfortably and then looked Bart in the eye. "My . . . Dieter, he was the fourth man." Clearing his throat, Axel continued. "The man that led your horses away told me after you had left.

You have already killed my . . . my son."

Bart felt a hot flash run through his body. He had been drunk and didn't even remember shooting him. "Well then, Axel, we have nothing to fight over. You believe in an eye for an eye."

"I said I would face you and kill you for my son. I don't have a choice. I'll let you take the coat off to keep it fair."

"Mr. Gerber, if you are looking to have me kill you to take away your pain, it's wrong. Me or you dying won't bring Dieter or Millie back. Those that done this, have paid. It is now our job to carry their memories, however painful they are."

Clearing his throat again, Axel seemed to sag. Within just moments he looked old and broken. "How do we do that?"

"Boss Bart, Mr. Gerber, you do it by keeping the good memories alive. A body can't live on hate." It was Joshua. He stood holding his hat in his hands and looking at the ground.

Glaring at the black man for a second, Axel turned and climbed into his saddle. The old man had regained some of his poise. Looking at Bart he said, "Maybe he is right." Turning his horse, he stopped. "There is one more man. The one that led your horses away. He told me about Dieter. He says he met you once. His name is Lonnie. My boy told him it was for a joke."

"Is he still at your ranch?" Bart asked.

"He is, and he is scared. Every time a stranger comes riding in he goes into hiding."

"Axel, you needn't tell him, but I won't come looking for the man. If I should meet him on the street, I can't say what will happen."

Axel Gerber sat on his horse and looked at the tall, rough man. "Fair enough." With that, he turned his horse and rode away.

"I am sorry for speaking my mind, Boss Bart. I jest couldn't help myself," Joshua said.

Bart put his arm over the black man's shoulders as they headed for the bunkhouse. "You were right. I will try and remember the good times."

CHAPTER TWENTY

Samuel and Joshua stayed busy with the cattle. Bart spent his days on the buckskin riding around the ranch, looking for nothing in particular. Every evening he sat on a rickety stool near Millie's grave. Sara brought him some coffee one evening and she could hear him talking to the dearly departed. Well after dark he would go into the barn and sleep in a bunk he'd put in the tack room. Since he'd been back, he hadn't set foot in the bunkhouse side he'd shared with Millie.

A month after coming back, Joshua met Bart heading from the barn to the well to wash up. The big man was still sporting the beard and long hair. "Boss Bart. I'll be going into Waco for a few things. Can I get anything for you?"

Bart looked up. His face was haggard from sleepless nights. "I ain't been of much use here," he said. "Make up a list and I'll go."

"Will you be taking the wagon?" Joshua asked.

"Yes. Yes, I think I will," Bart replied.

It had been night when the big man had tried to take Millie to the doctor. It was bright sunshine and warm as he drove the wagon, his head hanging down. Suddenly a chill went through his body. Bart's head jerked up and he realize he was passing the spot where she had died.

"I miss you so damn much," he mumbled as he slapped the team with the reins to hurry them along.

He pulled up to the livery in Waco. The hostler was taking in the sunshine on a scarred chair in the front. "I'll be in town a couple hours, Junior," Bart called, "would you give these nags some grain?"

Rocking forward as he stood up, Junior replied, "It'll be two bits. I won't even have to unhitch them."

Climbing down from the wagon, Bart waved and headed for the mercantile. Walking up the dusty street, the big man clutched the list. He felt physically drained. He passed the doc's office and even thought for a minute about stopping in and seeing if he could give him something to help him sleep.

Tom Cadwell was dusting off some pots and pans on a back shelf. At the sound of the chimes on the door, he quickly returned to the front. "You look like a damn grizzly with all that hair."

"I been meaning to shave and cut the hair, but I've been too damn busy," Bart lied.

"What can I get for you?" the merchant asked.

Setting the list down on the counter, the big man said, "Fill this for me. Maybe I'll go see that barber."

A portly man with slicked back hair and a impeccably trimmed moustache ran the barber shop and bath house. The place was empty when Bart walked in. "You're in the right place, stranger. A haircut and a trim of the beard is four bits."

"I ain't no stranger, Jelly," Bart snorted. "Haircut and a clean shave. If you got water heated, I'll have a bath."

"Got the hot water, Bart" Jelly replied. "I

didn't recognize you with all that hair. Six bits including the bath."

The deft hands of the barber quickly removed the beard and trimmed the hair. Brushing the last of the clippings from Bart' shoulders, he said, "You almost look human again. I'll get your bath poured."

Bart glanced at himself in the mirror. He shook his head as he headed for the bath. *I look like hell.*

The warm bath soothed the big man's tired body. Soon his tired eyes grew heavy and he began to doze. "It's been a damn hour!" Jelly yelled toward the back.

Bart's eyes opened with a start. The bath was now cold and his hands and feet were wrinkled from soaking in the water. The big man reached for the towel on the floor and stood up to dry off. "I'll be right out," he called back to the barber.

As they settled up Bart said, "I ain't been sleeping very good. That warm bath took me right out."

"Truth is, I got tired of your snoring and finally woke you," Jelly told him. "I sometimes have trouble getting to sleep. A nice, stiff shot of rye does the trick every time."

The hat felt loose as Bart set it onto his new haircut. He left the shop feeling surprisingly rested. It had been a long time since he had slept that sound. Passing the Mustang Saloon, he stopped and thought for a second before going in. He decided to pick up a few bottles to take back to the ranch. A shot in the evening just might do the trick for him.

* * *

It was six days later when Joshua came out of the bunkhouse and saw the wagon and team standing near Millie's grave. He set the coffee cup he was carrying on the bench near the door and ran to the wagon. Across the grave, crushing the flowers, lay Bart, passed out.

Joshua rolled the big man over. His face was bruised and his clothing was torn and filthy. He smelled of vomit and rye. Bart opened his eyes. "Where . . . where the hell am I?"

"Your killing Millie's flowers, Boss," Joshua said, then concern showed on his face. "Where have you been? It's over a week since you went to Waco."

"A week?" Bart asked. "I got the supplies and headed for Wolfgang's to spend the night."

Samuel had taken over the side of the bunkhouse where Bart and Millie had stayed. He came and stood by the wagon, a bewildered look on his face.

Leaving the big man on the ground, Joshua went to check the wagon. The goods he had requested were bagged and sitting in the back. Several empty rye bottles lay on the wagon floor. There was a note fastened to one of the bags.

If you come across this wagon send it to the Dabney ranch. Do not wake up the drunken driver.
Wolfgang

Sara came out of the bunkhouse and stood near the wagon, shock showing on her face. "Boss has been on a drunk," Joshua told her.

Collecting herself, Sara told her husband, "You

and Samuel get him down to the barn and clean him up before the children see him. I'll make something to eat."

Joshua watched her head back to the bunkhouse, worried lines on her face. The two men helped Bart stand and had him hang on to the side of the wagon as the team was led to the barn. Once Bart was inside Samuel started to put up the team while Joshua helped Bart sit on a nail keg. He then went to get a bucket of water from the well.

By the time Sara brought the bowl of porridge to the barn, Joshua had Bart cleaned up and dressed in fresh clothing. "You want me to feed you, Mister Bart?" she offered.

He reached for the bowl of hot cereal, his hand shaking. "Let me, please," she said. After she had fed him a few spoonfuls, the big man turned, went to his knees and began to vomit.

Sara set the bowl down on the floor and looked at her husband. "Help me get him into the bunk. If the children ask, Mister Bart caught some kind of sickness in town."

Tears were running down Sara's face as Samuel and Joshua helped Bart to the bunk. "Losing Millie is going to kill him," she whispered.

It was late afternoon before Bart emerged from the barn. Any evidence of the rye bottles was gone and his dirty clothes were soaking to be washed before mending. Joshua was pitching hay to the horses. Samuel had taken a horse to the corn field.

Bart walked up and leaned on a corral pole, watching Joshua work for a while. Setting down the fork, the black employee said, "Me and Samuel got the branding done and started plowing for the corn."

"How long was I gone?" Bart asked.

Shifting uncomfortably, Joshua said, "It weren't so long." Perking up, he added, "Sara has chicken soup for supper."

"What is today?" Bart repeated.

"You was gone just over a week," Joshua informed him. "We was just about to come looking for you and there you was, on top of Millie's grave."

"Thank you for telling me," the big man said. "I look forward to the soup." With that Bart walked over to the grave, set the stool upright and sat down.

Standing near the corral, Joshua couldn't hear what Bart was saying, but he was having a serious discussion with Millie.

That night, Bart joined Joshua family and Samuel for supper. She had chicken soup and corn bread. The big man was very hungry. He was unsure when he had last eaten. Nate and Mary were excited to see Bart. "I am glad you are feeling better," the young girl told him.

A smile broke out on Bart's rugged face. "I am glad to be back and seeing you all makes me feel much better."

With the meal finished, Bart and Joshua drank coffee on the bench in front of the bunkhouse while Samuel went to check on the stock. "I've made a decision," the big man said.

"What would that be?" Joshua asked.

"I am leaving the farm and going north," Bart said. "I would like you and your family to come with me. Samuel too."

"Where north?" Joshua asked.

"Kansas is a free territory. There is a fort named Riley that could use our beef, or if you want, you could ranch up there."

"The cattle are yours, Boss Bart. If you go, we must also go," the black said.

"The cattle are as much yours as mine," Bart said. "You are a free man. If you want to stay in Texas, I will leave the cattle here with you. The trip north would have its dangers and I can't make you go, but in Kansas your family would be free in a free territory."

Almost afraid to say the next words, Joshua decided to do so anyway. "What did Millie say?"

Bart looked at the grave and then back at Joshua with a half-smile on his face, "You heard me talking with her. She thinks it's a good idea." Then his face became serious. "She also said if I stay in Texas the drink will kill me."

The decision was made to go north to Fort Scott and plans were made for the trip. They had 187 cattle and six horses. They would need a few more horses and supplies for the trip. Additional repairs to strengthen the wagon, plus putting on a canvas cover, would be required.

When they had told Sara and the children about the trip, there was the look of fear on her face, but excitement on the children's. The children didn't consider the danger of the trip and the unknown of a new place. Joshua would have to spend a lot of time reassuring her.

Bart announced, "I will be going into Waco to get some additional horses and some supplies."

Quickly, Joshua said, "I will go with you to help with the horses."

"I would like you and Samuel to go with me," Bart said. For the first time since Sara had been told about the trip, she smiled.

Waco was busy as the three men drove down the crowded street. There was excitement in the air and it was all about gold. News of the California gold strike had reached the area a year ago and several men had dropped everything and headed west with a dream of riches. One of the men had been Newt Williams. A letter had just been received from the former Waco resident and he had struck it rich.

Gold fever had hit this part of Texas. A caravan of wagons, mules, horses, and men on foot carrying what they could on their backs had organized and was about to embark on the almost 2,000-mile trip to get a share of the wealth. There was an urgency to get started, to beat the snow in the mountains.

Bart was not able to park the wagon anywhere near the mercantile, so he pulled in behind the livery. Junior rushed to meet them. "Folks in town have gone crazy," he said gleefully. "That good-for-nothing, Newt Williams, found gold in California and now the whole damn town wants to head west."

"Hell, I thought they was going to hang someone important to bring folks in like this," Bart kidded.

"I can get you a good price for that there wagon and top dollar for your horses," Junior said.

The big man shook his head, "They're not for sale. I plan to relocate myself. I am just in town to pick up some supplies and then we're heading for Kansas."

"You won't find any supplies in Cadwell's," the hostler informed him. "Them crazy galoots bought everything off his shelves for twice what they was worth."

This was a small setback for Bart, because he

was planning to drive cattle north and could get what he needed in any of the many towns he'd come across before the Red River. Once he crossed the river and got into Indian Territory, places to get supplies would be few and far between.

Bart had hoped to purchase a few more horses from Junior, but now that would not happen. He turned to Joshua, "You stay here with Samuel and watch our wagon and stock." He handed him the Hawken. "Use this if you have to if anyone tries to take them."

"I can't kill one of these town folk," Joshua told him.

"In that case, just fire it in the air and I'll come running." With that, Bart headed into the excited crowd in town.

He quickly learned that the caravan was leaving at first light tomorrow. Not only had they bought out the mercantile, but they had also purchased every bottle from the Mustang Saloon. Up and down the street were men celebrating the coming venture for riches. By the looks of some of the partiers, the morning would come and go without any knowledge of them.

Tony was sitting on the porch in front of the saloon. Bart took a chair next to him. "It looks like a good day for Waco," the big man said.

The bartender chuckled, "I got my try for gold in the Chattahoochee River in Georgia back in '29. I was just a kid back then. After a couple of months, I was broke and was starving. I sold my boots and belt to buy enough food to leave. Then, barefoot and holding my pants up, I walked 200 miles back to my father's farm."

"That's a damn good hard luck story," Bart replied. "If they live through the trip, most of these poor bastards will have one to beat yours."

"I got a little beer left if you want a mug," Tony said.

"I best not," the big man said. "I haven't sweat out the drunk yet. Right now, I don't even trust beer."

All of a sudden there was a rifle shot. "Damn!" Bart exclaimed, as he ran toward the livery.

He rounded the back to the livery to find Joshua and Samuel standing in the back of the wagon and three men unhitching the team. One was laughing, "They sure are dumb. Shooting the only bullet into the air."

Bart grabbed the man nearest to him by the back of the hair and swung him against the livery wall, knocking him out cold. Then he snapped at the other two, "You best get them animals hitched back up before I send you both to Hell!"

The two men turned to look down the barrel of the Dragoon in Bart's hand. They could see their partner in crime lying on the ground next to the livery. "We . . . we didn't mean nothing," the short stocky thief stammered. "We was just kidding with your blacks."

With hands shaking the two men got the horses hitched to the wagon and then began to back away from the big man glaring at them. "Grab that son-of-a-bitch and take him with you," Bart said, motioning with the Colt.

He looked up at Joshua and Samuel in the wagon as he slipped the Dragoon back into his holster. "You did good. Get the team watered and then we'll leave. I'll go and see if Tony has any cheese and bread to take with us."

The big man pushed his way through the throng of men in the street. He stepped up onto the saloon porch and came face to face with Lonnie, who was sipping on a mug of beer. The young man's eyes grew large. His hand shook and he dropped the mug, splashing beer across the porch.

For a second Bart was confused, then he remembered the young man and his tall friend coming to the ranch looking for work. This young man in need of a shave was Lonnie, the man who had led his horses from the corral.

"We meet again," Bart said coldly.

"I . . . I ain't afraid of you mister," Lonnie said, his hand hovering above his holster.

"You should be," Bart snapped. "You're standing there about to wet yourself and the loop is on your gun."

The young man's eyes were wild. He was trapped and expected to die in the next few seconds. "I didn't know what they was planning," he pleaded. Suddenly he raised both of his hands. "If you shoot me they will hang you."

Glaring at the young man, Bart asked, "Are you joining these fools heading for the gold fields?"

Suddenly there was hope on Lonnie's face. "I leave come morning."

"The Comancheros or the mountains will probably kill you," Bart said. "I don't need to waste a bullet. Now get the hell out of my sight."

The young man took off like a shot, disappearing into the crowded street. Bart walked into the saloon. Tony was standing at the end of the bar. "He's a good kid. I'm glad you didn't kill him."

"He was lucky his loop was on the gun and it give me time to think," the big man admitted. "Can I get some grub for my men and me for the trip back to the ranch?"

CHAPTER TWENTY ONE

It was late June 1850 and all was ready to drive the cattle north. Sara and Samuel would take turns driving the covered wagon. Mary, being only eight, would walk or ride with her mother. Nathaniel, big for a ten year-old, would be riding a horse and help with driving the herd.

After getting back from Waco, Bart and Joshua had made a trip to the Collins ranch. Henry had been willing to sell Bart the horses he needed. He had been sorry to hear that they were relocating to Kansas. Too many ranchers had given up, finding it difficult to get decent money for their cattle. Henry Collins had even offered to help Bart start sheep ranching if he'd stay.

Fort Scott was a bit less than 600 miles from Waco. It would take just over two months to drive the herd north. Bart spent the last morning sitting near Millie's grave. The night before he had had a dream of her. She had walked up to him and kissed him goodbye. The dream had been so real that Bart could swear that she had been there.

He said his final goodbye by placing his hand on the headstone. The morning sun was shining on the stones engraving.

Here Lies Our Love
Bartholomew and Millie
Nevell
1849

It was a warm June day when they pushed the herd off the ranch. Nate rode on the left flank while Bart took up drag. Joshua pushed the extra horses and watched the right flank. The wagon took the lead with Samuel handling the reins. Sara stood near the seat, watching the ranch building disappear. She wondered if her family would ever have another home.

Fort Worth had been established on Clear Fork the prior November. It had been named after General William Worth. The fort was on their route and Bart planned to purchase supplies there. The first day barely got them past Waco. Bart had swung by Wolfgang's to wish his old friend farewell.

The cattle were still full of energy and tended to wander while grazing. Bart and Joshua were kept busy pushing them back until after dark. Samuel came out to ride herd and give the two men a chance to have a bite to eat and get some rest. Sara had kept the thick chicken soup warm near the fire and had some day-old bread.

Being shorthanded, Bart planned to have three three-hour turns riding herd at night. The first being from 9 to 12. That would cover the hours of darkness. The herd would be pushed up to 20 miles a day until they crossed the Red River. After that, they would go 10 to 12 miles a day.

Bart had it all planned out, but he couldn't control the weather or other outside influences. The next day they got an early start. The weather was holding and water was still plentiful. It would be four days to Fort Worth, and then another four days to the Red River. Just a year ago, Bart had ridden this way from Fort Leavenworth. Knowledge from that trip would help them avoid many of the trouble spots.

The only breaks the men got during the day was when they were switching horses. Samuel would take over for Nate and let him ride in the wagon part of the day while Sara drove. They were all exhausted by the time they reached Fort Worth.

The fort was a cluster of buildings surrounding a parade ground. It had been established like so many others to protect the residence from Indian attacks. While Joshua and Samuel watched the herd, Bart took the wagon in to get supplies. Nate and Mary watched wide-eyed as they crossed Clear Fork into the fort. They were met by a lieutenant who was in charge of the commissary. Bart pulled the team to a stop.

"I am Lieutenant Kent, the fort's quartermaster," the man introduced himself. "I see you are pushing some cattle. Will you be setting up in this area?"

Climbing off of the wagon, Bart stood tall and looked down on the sharply dressed lieutenant. "We're just passing through. We need supplies for our trip north."

"I can help you with the supplies," Lieutenant Kent replied. "Maybe you can help me. We could use some beef and wondered it you had any to sell."

Bart had dealt with the army long enough to know that the man was just being polite asking if they had any to sell. If he said no, then the army would just take a few or the whole herd. They would pay for them, but the plans for a ranch in Kansas would be gone.

"We have some we could spare," Bart told the quartermaster. "How many would you need."

The lieutenant stared at the herd across Clear Fork. "Can you spare 10 at $15 a piece?"

"Well," Bart pondered, "In Kansas, Fort Scott will pay $20, maybe a little more."

The quartermaster furled his brow, thinking. "Considering you won't have to drive them north, how about $18?"

Bart reached out and shook the lieutenant's hand. "It's a deal."

Once back with the wagon and the supplies, Bart and Joshua cut out 10 of the older longhorn steers and drove them to the fort. "These are going to be tough chewing," Joshua said.

"The army has strong teeth," Bart replied, smiling. "They won't mind."

The big man had planned to rest a day at the fort, but decided to move on north before the quartermaster tried to dicker them out of more cows. Several times as they traveled, they would catch sight of riders a distance from the herd, watching them. Bart let the others know that they'd best stay alert on night watch. The biggest danger was having horses stolen.

A stiff wind was blowing the day they reached the Red River. It made the churning river look even more formidable. They set up camp on the south bank with the hope that the wind would die during the night. Bart had told young Nate that he'd be crossing in the wagon.

After a simple supper of johnnycakes and coffee. Sara had mixed in some molasses to make them sweet. Nate was sitting against the wagon wheel and picking at his johnnycake. "Not hungry tonight?" Bart asked him.

"I'm thinking," the boy replied, staring at his food.

The big man moved closer to him. "It kinda looks like you were thinking serious thoughts."

Nate looked at Bart, his brown eyes somber. "I'm a good rider and I learned to swim two years ago. I can ride a horse across the river and help with the cattle on the other side."

Bart smiled at Nate. As the young man spoke, he tended to sit up straighter and had the look of determination on his face. "If your father says it is okay for you to ride across," Bart said, "it is okay with me."

Like a shot, Nate was off to see his father.

* * *

Bart had chosen a crossing that would only require swimming for a short distance. Most of the way, the water would be belly-deep on the horses. The current would push the cattle, horses, and wagon downstream. The wind had not slackened.

Samuel would be driving the wagon across while Sara and Mary would stay in the wagon. Their supplies were piled to keep items that could be damaged by the water on top. The roiling water would splash up against the sides of the wagon and animals, making the river seem deeper.

The banks and cliffs along the river were red dirt and stone. Samuel and the wagon went first. Halfway across the wagon floated and swung downstream. The team swam frantically for the far shore, being hampered by the floating anchor behind them. Samuel shouted and slapped them with the reins to keep them going. Suddenly, the left horse stumbled as its hooves hit bottom. It bumped against the right horse, and for a moment panic set in, with the horses struggling to gain their footing while Samuel and Sara shouted for all they were worth to encourage them to continue. Then the wagon wheels made contact with the bottom and, after some jerking and rocking, the wagon was on sound footing and once again under control.

Bart, Joshua, and Nate sat on their horses, helpless to do anything to help as they watched the wagon. Relief flooded over them when the wagon made the other side. Pulling his horse around, Bart shouted, "We now know what the river will be like. Let's get them cows in the water."

Some of the cattle were hesitant to enter the river and kept Bart and Joshua busy pushing them back toward the river. Nate went in with the first bunch, riding upstream of the cattle. Clinging to the mane of his horse, and waving his hat to keep the animals going, he made it across without any problem. Once across he began to push those on the other side away from the bank to make room for the remaining plunging cattle as they came ashore.

Joshua brought up the back of the herd crossing and could not have been prouder of his son as he watched the lad work. Nathaniel was a born cowboy. While the cattle were being settled down on the north side of the river, Sara and Mary had set up camp and were busy unloading the wagon to dry items that had gotten wet. Samuel was gathering some scrub wood to get a fire going.

They were now in the Indian Territory. The cattle would be crossing land controlled by Cherokee, Creek, Chickasaw, Choctaw, and Seminole. They were known as the Five Civilized Tribes. While civilized, they were not beyond stealing horses, or taking a cow or two for the right of crossing their land.

Bart estimated that it would take three weeks to cross the Indian Territory. They were not far from where he had lost his packhorse coming down to find Millie. They would be traveling through rolling plains, which would offer plenty of cover for anyone watching their herd. While watching for any riders, Bart would often see small herds of buffalo.

A week into the territory Joshua rode around the back of the herd to the right flank where Bart was riding. "We got someone following us," he told the big man.

"Might be the Chickasaw that stole my packhorse," Bart replied.

"It ain't an Indian, Boss. He's riding a rose gray. I saw him once in Texas and again this morning."

"Are you sure it was the same rider?" the big man asked.

"It was early morning and he was away off, so I can't be sure the man was the same, but the pinkish gray he was riding was," Joshua replied.

"It would be unlikely that there'd be two rose grays around," Bart agreed.

The rider remained a mystery for another week as they crossed the territory. Two Choctaw rode up to the herd and had demanded two horses for payment of driving the cattle across their land. Bart held firm and debated with the two using sign language. He was finally able to get them to settle for three longhorns.

The big man left the negotiations with an uncomfortable feeling that they might come back in the dark and take the two horses. He only hoped that if they did, they'd bring back the cows.

Samuel was riding herd and the sun was just breaking over the eastern horizon when he galloped to the camp. "Massa Bart!" he yelled. "Two men coming and one is on the rose gray."

Bart was sitting on his blankets, pulling on his boots. He stood up, strapping on his holster. Sara was still in the wagon, getting the children up, and Joshua was building the cook fire. The two riders came around the wagon and stopped in front of Bart.

The man on the rose gray smiled. "Sorry to come into your camp unannounced, but I believe we got some business to discuss."

The second man sat quietly with his rifle across the front of his saddle, aimed in the general direction of Bart. Samuel had joined Joshua near the fire. Sara stayed out of sight in the wagon.

"I don't believe I know you, mister," Bart replied. "I don't believe we have anything to discuss."

"You should know that this here is a lawman out of Missouri and I got papers on the runaways you got here," the man said, no longer smiling.

"Just who the hell are you?" Bart demanded.

"Tip Hanson's the name, and I represent the estate of Jedidiah Heller. I got a warrant sworn by his aunt," the man said, his face taking on the look of meanness.

"We are no longer in Texas, so the warrant is no good," Bart snapped. "Smoke stole these blacks off my ranch. I got papers from Charles Dabney giving them their freedom and they are registered in Waco."

"Like you said," Tip replied, "we are no longer in Texas and my warrant is good wherever I find the runaways. I got proof they are runaways and you are helping them. U.S. Marshal Goody is here to take them back to Missouri, where they will be sold and the proceeds will be sent to Mrs. Heller."

Disbelief over what was happening was replaced by anger in the big man. "I would like to see your warrant," Bart requested, trying to buy time while he figured out what to do.

Suddenly, Marshal Goody spoke up. "The warrant states that Joshua, Sara, and two children were the property of Jedidiah Heller and were taken from Mrs. Heller's holding area. Mr. Heller has disappeared and is believed to be the victim of foul play."

Bart decided that he would show the U.S. Marshal the papers he had and then if Tip Hanson was allowed to take the family, he was going to kill them both or die trying. The big man went to his saddlebags and pulled out the documents. He handed them to the marshal.

"Smoke, or Jedidiah as you call him, stole slaves off the Dabney place and then sold them using false papers," Bart said. "He also was involved in a rape and beating of a woman I was to marry. Millie ended up dying as a result."

"For all I know, Hanson here might have been a partner of Smoke's. He might have even killed him," the big man added, trying to discredit Tip.

All of a sudden, Tip became angry. "Damn you, Goody. I brung you out here to haul these damn runaways back to Missouri. I am owed money for each one I catch."

The marshal folded Bart's documents and

handed them back. "I am the law in the Indian Territory and sworn to bring in those that break them," Marshal Goody said. "I ain't a judge and each of you have papers that don't agree with one another. I don't much care for having to ride all the way out here on this damn property claim. You will have to go back to Texas and sort this out."

The marshal began to turn his horse away. Without warning, Tip pulled his gun and shot Goody. He then turned the gun toward Bart. His eyes went big when he saw the Dragoon lined up on him. Fire belched from the Colt, knocking Tip from his saddle. As he hit the ground, Bart put another shot into him.

He then ran to the aid of the marshal. The bullet had gone in behind the arm and had torn a long gash across his back. Sara climbed out of the wagon holding a Paterson revolver. "Get some water heating!" Bart shouted.

The big man got the marshal sitting up and, with the help of Joshua, got his shirt off. Samuel brought some strips of cloth and Bart wrapped them around Goody to try and stop the bleeding. They all worked on the wounded marshal while ignoring the dead runaway hunter lying a short distance away.

Once the marshal was bandaged, Bart went to the fire. Sara had coffee and johnnycakes ready. She looked at the big man. "I was going to kill him when he came to the wagon to get me," she said. "When we were brought to the cages, I saw him. He liked hurting people."

"Well, Tip Hanson won't be hurting anyone else," Bart said. "I wasn't sure about my first shot, but the second one sure as hell killed him."

The marshal traveled with the herd for four

days before they came to a Creek village. Goody was familiar with some of the residents and chose to stay in the village until he was able to ride back to Missouri. Marshal Goody was civil traveling with Bart and the blacks, but insisted on riding his horse and only conversed with Bart.

He did give the rose gray horse and, most of Hanson's gear to Bart. Tim Hanson had no epitaph, just an unmarked grave and the clothes he'd died in. The group was relieved to get rid of the U.S. Marshal. There was always the lingering fear that he would change his mind and decide to bring Joshua and his family to Missouri.

There was no sign or markers when the herd entered the Kansas Territory. When they finally passed a small trading post and the owner declared that he lived in Kansas, Samuel broke into a broad smile. "I is in a free territory."

* * *

Fort Scott had been built to protect emigrants settling in the territory. It was located just west of the Missouri boarder. The fort consisted of stone buildings and a mix of wooden structures. Bart set up camp on a stream just west of the fort. While Joshua and Samuel settled the cattle down, he rode to the fort.

The major recognized Bart. His first question was, "Are you ready to come back to the army? We need scouts, or I can probably get you a commission."

"I thank you, Major," Bart replied. "I am not sure what my next move will be. If it is the army I will let you know."

"What can I do for you?" the major asked.

"I got a family of blacks that have a small herd we drove up from Texas. They were freed by a man named Charles Dabney. I was hoping they could do some ranching near here."

"I got to warn you," the major said, "we have had trouble with some from Missouri that come over and don't think blacks should be free. We have been able to keep the trouble down, but the soldiers can't be everywhere."

"It should be better than being in Texas," Bart replied.

"There's a place about four hours west," the major said. "A fellow was killed by a fall and his wife and children went east. The place is proved up some and I can provide papers allowing your folks to ranch there."

"I'll let Joshua know," the big man said. "He will have cattle to sell if you need any to feed your soldiers."

"We can always use the meat," the major said. "Have him see the quartermaster."

It was four days before the cattle were driven to the abandoned farm. The house consisted of three rooms and there was a small barn and corral. A small river ran near the farm, providing needed water and a place for Nate to do some fishing.

While at the fort, Bart had registered the herd and extra horses in Joshua's name. The big man promised Sara that he'd stay until they were settled in. After that, Bart knew that too many memories had traveled with them from Texas, and a day didn't go by that he didn't ache for Millie.

There were large cottonwoods providing shade near the farm and Bart would set up a camp for himself under them. Once the day's work was done, he would watch the sunset. Samuel would join him some evenings. "I can almost see heaven from here," he'd say.

They were saddened one morning when they found that Samuel had gone to his maker while he slept. He was buried deep near the grave of the farmer. Bart made sure that there was a stone marker.

The big man now realized that his quest for revenge and leaving Texas had not eased the pain he carried over the loss of Millie. He knew that he had done wrong when he'd found Jonny. The others, well, maybe the West was safer without them. With Joshua settled on the farm, there was nothing keeping Bart in Kansas.

He bid farewell to the family. Mounting his horse and his packs on the rose gray, he sat unsure of the direction he should go. Slowly, he turned Buck. With little urging the horse moved out. Bart rode west, into the sunset, remembering Joshua's words, think of the good times he and Millie had shared.

www.ingramcontent.com/pod-product-compliance
Lightning Source LLC
Chambersburg PA
CBHW072223170626
46813CB00003B/1068